"Tomozaki-kun, you're really good at *Atafami*, huh?"

Aoi Hinami

"What if my chastity is in danger?!"

Minami Nanami

"You and Aoi sure are friendly these days, aren't you, Tomozaki-kun?"

Yuzu Izumi

CONTENTS

Fumiya Tomozaki

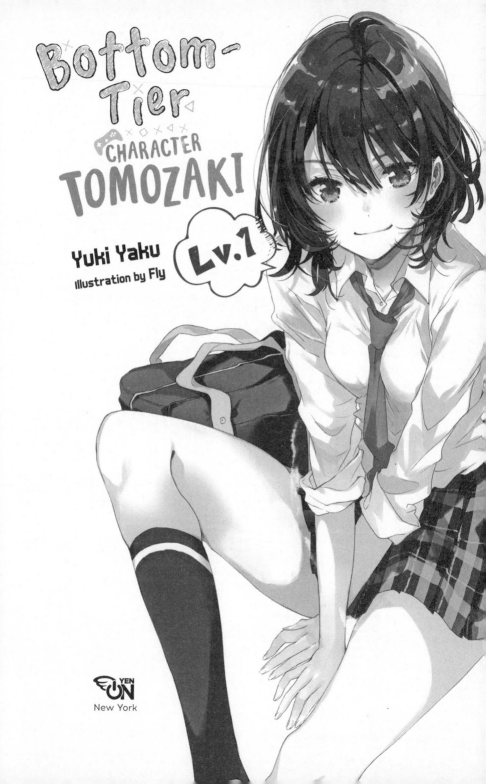

Bottom-Tier
Character
TOMOZAKI

Yuki Yaku

Illustration by Fly

Lv.1

YEN ON
New York

YUKI YAKU

Cover art by Fly
Translation by Winifred Bird

JAKU CHARA TOMOZAKI-KUN LV.1
by Yuki YAKU
© 2016 Yuki YAKU
Illustration by FLY
All rights reserved.
Original Japanese edition published by SHOGAKUKAN.
English translation rights in the United States of America, Canada, the United Kingdom, Ireland, Australia, and New Zealand arranged with SHOGAKUKAN through Tuttle-Mori Agency, Inc.

English translation © 2019 by Yen Press, LLC

Yen On
150 West 30th Street, 19th Floor
New York, NY 10001

Visit us at yenpress.com
facebook.com/yenpress
twitter.com/yenpress
yenpress.tumblr.com
instagram.com/yenpress

First Yen On Edition: July 2019

Yen On is an imprint of Yen Press, LLC.
The Yen On name and logo are trademarks of Yen Press, LLC.

The publisher is not responsible for websites (or their content) that are not owned by the publisher.

Library of Congress Cataloging-in-Publication Data
Names: Yaku, Yuki, author. | Fly, 1963- illustrator. | Bird, Winifred, translator.
Title: Bottom-tier character Tomozaki / Yuki Yaku ; illustration by Fly ; translation by Winifred Bird.
Other titles: Jaku chara Tomozaki-kun. English
Description: First Yen On edition. | New York : Yen On, 2019-
Identifiers: LCCN 2019017466 | ISBN 9781975358259 (v. 1 ; pbk.)
Subjects: LCSH: Video games–Fiction. | Video gamers–Fiction.
Classification: LCC PL877.5.A35 J9313 2019 | DDC 895.63/6–dc23
LC record available at https://lccn.loc.gov/2019017466

ISBN: 978-1-9753-5825-9

10 9 8 7 6 5 4 3 2 1

LSC-C

Printed in the United States of America

Bottom-Tier CHARACTER TOMOZAKI

Characters

Fumiya Tomozaki
Second-year high school student. Bottom-tier.

Aoi Hinami
Second-year high school student. Perfect heroine of the school.

Minami Nanami
Second-year high school student. Class clown.

Hanabi Natsubayashi
Second-year high school student. Small.

Yuzu Izumi
Second-year high school student. Hot.

Fuka Kikuchi
Second-year high school student. Bookworm.

Common Honorifics

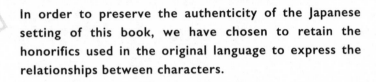

In order to preserve the authenticity of the Japanese setting of this book, we have chosen to retain the honorifics used in the original language to express the relationships between characters.

No honorific: Indicates familiarity or closeness; if used without permission or reason, addressing someone in this manner would constitute an insult.

-san: The Japanese equivalent of Mr./Mrs./Miss. If a situation calls for politeness, this is the fail-safe honorific.

-kun: Used most often when referring to boys, this indicates affection or familiarity. Occasionally used by older men among their peers, but it may also be used by anyone referring to a person of lower standing.

-chan: An affectionate honorific indicating familiarity used mostly in reference to girls; also used in reference to cute persons or animals of either gender.

0

I always feel kind of down when I watch
the opening after I beat a game

"Life is a god-tier game." I know there's that famous copypasta about it, but if you ask me, it's a bunch of crap.

Only people who've never been in a genuinely shitty situation would think the world is actually balanced to let you clear each level by the skin of your teeth with a little skill and effort. You think every character you'll meet has a deep backstory? That's just a stale fantasy you'll hear from people who have no idea how many shallow mobs are out there.

It's not necessarily a great thing to live in $\infty \times \infty$ HD and and ∞ frames per second. After all, some things are interesting only when their pixel count is low. The reason ugly guys like me look so ugly is the resolution around here is too high. I'm sure I'd look more like everyone else if the world was made of pixel art. Oh, I'm not crying over it or anything.

But even before we get into that, it's wrong to think that complexity and pizzazz necessarily make something good. The best games are always the simple and beautiful ones.

That's true for *shogi*, and it's true for *Super Mario*. All the latest FPSs have simple rules and concepts. Depth and flavor thrive within those simple rules and concepts.

All the games that go down in history are like that.

So how does real life measure up?

Since ancient times, tons of brilliant scientists have been conducting experiments to search for a Law of Everything that explains the rules of our world. They still haven't found it.

Since ancient times, tons of brilliant philosophers have been wrapping ideas up in logic trying to figure out the meaning of life—in other words, life's concept. You can just argue the meaning is different for each person. I've never heard a single good comeback for it.

If you forced me to come up with the basic rules and concept for how life really is, I can only think of one, and it's not exactly simple: Just live. Beyond that, you're on your own. What's so great about a game like that?

Not to mention that even if you act like everyone else, you get discriminated against or treated badly because of your face or your build or your age. No matter how hard you try, if you get sick when it's time to play, you lose everything. All I can see are convincing reasons to call life a shitty game. Bottom-tier characters like me haven't committed any crimes. We're just tyrannized because we happen to have been born weak.

It's absurd and unfair. The world is stacked against the weak.

Ergo, shitty game.

It's a commonplace cliché, but it fits the real world perfectly.

Sure, some people might argue with me. "You probably think that because you're not trying hard enough at life," they'll say. It's just the kind of skewed comment you'd expect from someone born into this world as a top-tier character.

They don't notice life's ridiculous requirements because they start out at an advantage. They mistakenly assume that maining a top-tier character and dominating on easy mode is fun, and that's all there is to life.

In other words, it's nothing more than the opinion of some noob gamer.

If you haven't mastered the game, you'd better step back.

If you're a noob who happens to have been born strong and has been taking it easy ever since, you don't have the right to talk about life.

I know what I'm talking about. I've worked hard at every kind of game there is, and I've been standing on the mountaintop for quite a while.

The game of life is garbage.

—nanashi, the best gamer in Japan

1

Say what you want, famous games are usually fun

It was obvious who was better.

Anyone could tell as much by watching the movements of my ninja, Found, and Nakamura's fox character, Foxy. Okay, I guess he wasn't terrible for a normie. Word was he'd been winning tons of bets with *Atafami*—the game we were playing—but now his real level was clear to see. I knew I'd win as soon as the game started.

Still, I'm not one to cut corners when it comes to *Atafami*. It didn't matter that Nakamura only had one stock left. My plan was to throw him off by pretending to charge straight at him like a madman, and then "wavedash." I figured that at his level, he probably didn't even know what wavedashing was—an advanced technique accomplished by short hopping and then immediately performing a directional air dodge diagonally into the ground to slide a short distance. With proper execution, the full technique happens in less than a second.

Nakamura fell for my feint and tried to hit me. I dodged by wavedashing backward and then seized the opportunity to approach. In this game, throws are the foundation of combos. It's all about how many combos you can pile on after starting with a throw. My character Found is really good at this.

Found grabbed Nakamura's character. After that, the game was mine. One after another I hit him with combos that looked easy but actually required delicate maneuvering. It's not that there was no way to break out—he just didn't know how. Naturally, it was over.

Nakamura was out of stocks.

"All righty, then."

Welp, I won. Not that there was any chance I would lose to an amateur in *Atafami*, but I was surprised by how easy it had been. What came next was the part I was worried about.

Each player starts with four stocks. You face off on a flat stage, no gimmicks, with someone you've never played before.

Those were the rules. They were fair, and now Nakamura had zero stocks left. Me? I had four. So yeah, I demolished him.

When I looked over at him, I could tell he wanted to say something. He kept glancing back and forth from my face to the controller in my hand, and I could make out the tiniest shade of an inferiority complex in his eyes. Kinda surprising, actually. During a normal day at school, Nakamura would never look at me with that weakness in his eyes. I hadn't expected this.

He was handsome, with dyed brown hair. You could tell at a glance he was one of those people who's good at real life—top of the class, a strong athlete, girls all over him, even good at video games. A smooth operator, head and shoulders above everyone around him.

You have the ever-confident Nakamura, normie extraordinaire, looking at me like a kicked puppy. At me—an extreme, in-your-face geek.

"…chose the wrong…" Nakamura was saying something.

"Huh?"

"I just chose the wrong character."

"…What?"

"I had a bad character. That's why I lost."

"Um, n-no, these two characters are in the same tier…"

"It's not that—it's about the matchup. It was just a bad match for yours," he tried to tell me matter-of-factly.

I was dumbfounded. That was just an excuse no matter how you slice it.

Then I realized what was going on. His stubborn refusal to accept defeat gracefully was a sign of just how much he looked down on me. Losing to me was so humiliating that this show was the only way he could hold onto his pride. He didn't even bother to make his excuse a good one. My inferiority was a given for him. This kind of injustice is commonplace when you're on the bottom-tier of life.

Except for moments like this.

For those moments when I was sitting in front of *Atafami*, things were different.

"A-actually, Foxy drops fast, so I'd have to say it's actually easier to do combos with him."

"I guess. It's all about the matchups with this game."

I took a breath and looked Nakamura straight in the eyes. I was scared. But…

"…That's just an excuse." I'm so used to people looking down on me, it doesn't even bother me that much.

"Look, I'm totally right, but you're all happy 'cause you won this shitty game. It's so dumb."

This, on the other hand, I'll never get used to. I can't stand it when someone gets stomped and then pretends they weren't even trying.

"Yeah, I am happy, and you only think it's dumb 'cause you lost. You've never experienced what it's like to win, so I wouldn't expect you to understand. I'd get it if you won and then said it was dumb, but you lost, and now you sound like a sore loser."

As far as I was concerned, we were on the battlefield of *Atafami*, and words were my ammo.

"Huh? It's all about which characters are better against others. God, this game sucks. Win or lose, it's shit."

"The matchup can't explain how much better I was. You lost because you're a weak player. I'd win even if we traded characters."

"…Fine. Let's switch characters. I can promise I'm not gonna lose to you again."

His eyes lit up with fighting spirit. Only people in the top tier of life have that kind of baseless confidence. The courage—or should I say the stupidity—to insist they'll never lose even in this situation. Bottom-tier characters like me don't have that privilege. We don't have the strength to act like we're right when we're wrong—the confidence to think, *Of course it'll work out. I'm me.* We lack that animalistic power.

In fact, it's the opposite—even though I had just crushed him, I still felt slightly uneasy for some reason.

But for that one moment, I wasn't bottom-tier.

"...Actually, this is gonna be annoying," I said.

"Come on. If you're that sure of yourself, play me again."

"It's not that. I just don't want to have to listen to your dumb excuses again after I beat you."

"Huh?"

When I'm playing *Atafami*, I'm a beast. "Fine. But we have to trade controllers, too. I don't want to listen to you tell me the buttons didn't work. Oh, and we should probably trade seats, 'cause you'd probably say something about the glare on the screen. Let's start with eight stocks, too. Long battles are where your strength really shows, right? What else? How about we ban combos your opponent can't get out of unless they know how? 'Cause that's really about knowledge more than skill, right? That should make it a pure competition of skill, reflexes, and decision-making ability. Did I forget anything? ...Oh, should we trade clothes?"

Ha-ha-ha. Welp, I sure told him. Man, was I ever going to regret this later.

"...Uh, no, we shouldn't. Don't be a dick, dude. Seriously."

That was a mean look he was giving me. When someone glares at me like that, I can't help reacting like prey meeting an animal higher on the food chain, and pretty soon I'm feeling so inferior I want to start apologizing. Even though in this case, there was no question I was in the right. Those are the rules of life.

Nakamura and I traded places, traded controllers, traded characters, each got eight lives, did not trade clothes, and then we were a start-button press away from the battle.

"If I win, you have to say it, Nakamura."

"I know that."

"I don't think you do."

"...No, I do. I'll say you're better."

"No, I mean—of course that, but there's something else you have to acknowledge."

"What?"

He just didn't get it.

"Earlier you said *Atafami* was a shitty game, right?"

"Huh?"

I was actually more pissed about that than about the fact that he wouldn't admit he lost.

"…You have to say that *Atafami* is god-tier."

Obviously, I eight-stocked him.

* * *

nanashi: gg
Koki: good game

The next day, I was playing online matches in *Attack Families*—which everyone calls *Atafami*. Since players can chat online with one another, it's considered polite to exchange a few words after the game. Of course, I had just won.

My winrate was going up steadily. After the rankings were reset four months earlier, I'd climbed to the number one spot in Japan in just a couple weeks and stayed there without any real threat ever since. My gaming handle is nanashi, which means no-name. I chose it because I was embarrassed to give myself a name, and plus "no-name" sounded cool. No connection to my real name, Fumiya Tomozaki.

Before the rates were reset, I'll admit, I dropped down the rankings a couple of times, but I was still almost always in the top spot. It would probably be accurate to say I don't have any real competition in Japan.

Atafami has more players than any other online PvP, thanks to its unusually high quality. In fact, if I'm the top player in this game, I might as well say I'm the best gamer in Japan. Maybe.

There's only one other *Atafami* player I pay attention to, partly because of their handle: NO NAME. They've never actually stolen my place as number one, but for the past couple of months they've been right there behind me at number two. This whole time, as far as I know, no one's stolen their place, either. In other words, nanashi and NO NAME have monopolized the top two spots.

In part because our names are so close, a false but plausible rumor has been going around the online gaming community that both accounts belong to the same person.

As nanashi himself, let me assure you right now. Nanashi and NO NAME are two completely different people.

Still, there is circumstantial evidence for the theory: the fact that NO NAME only appeared in the *Atafami* world a few months ago; the fact that they rocketed to second place at an impossible speed for someone so new; and most of all, the fact that nanashi and NO NAME have never competed head on. After all, we both use Found, and we seem to have similar playing styles. NO NAME probably learned from watching videos of me in the game archives.

nanashi: gg
Yukichi: gg. You're super good!
nanashi: Thanks. Bye.

Once again, I won and left the match. Sure, I still lose occasionally, but these days even that has started to take on aspects of a fight against myself. I never lose because of my opponent's skills—it's almost always because of a mistake on my side. That's why even at number one, it's still worth putting in effort. I can still say I have room to grow.

I had just been thinking that my next goal should be to reduce errors during fights when I glanced at the name written in the NEXT OPPONENT box and my breath caught in my throat.

NO NAME   Rating: 2561

I could feel my pulse starting to pound my head.

For the first time in ages, I was looking forward to a good fight. I could feel my grasp on the controller tightening.

"What are you talking about? That isn't even all of it. You talked to someone in home ec when I wasn't there. What did I tell you? Only do it when I'm nearby."

"No, that was…"

"Listen. This time, Nakamura butted in after I got there, so it worked out, but do you know what would have happened without me? Hanabi might have blown up, and you could have become a school joke. If that happened, you'd be getting further from, not closer to, achieving your goals."

"S-sorry… So the reason you told me to wait till you were there was so you could rescue me if something bad happened?"

"Obviously. If I just wanted to know you'd done it, I could ask the girls directly afterward or find out some other way."

"H-Hinami…"

She was so kind…

"You're not starting to think I care about you, are you? Because all I care about is my decision to help you achieve your goals, and I don't want all my work to be wasted."

"Oh right."

"Plus, it's not just so I can rescue you. I want to observe how the girls react when you talk to them, the kind of conversations you have, and your conversational skills before I decide where we go from here. I mean, before I decide who you become friends with and what kind of practice you do."

"You've thought through all that?"

"Obviously. If you're planning to take on a boss, you're not going to win unless your level is high enough for whatever they're going to throw at you."

"That…"

I was completely sincere.

"…is exactly right."

…Honestly, whenever we talked about games, we always saw eye to eye.

"Okay, then. As far as next steps…take off your mask for a minute."

"Uh, okay." I did as she said, and my huge smile finally saw the light of day.

"Try going back to your regular face again."

I followed her instructions.

"Hmm, I see. Your training is showing results."

"Huh?"

"Do you see it?"

"Whoa—"

She was holding out a hand mirror, and what I saw startled me. I thought I was making my default expression, but compared to the last time she shoved a mirror in front of my face, the area around my mouth definitely looked firmer.

"Even two days made a difference. You must have been working hard. Good job."

"Well, you told me to do it constantly."

"Yeah…you'll do fine. From now on, you don't have to do it all the time. You can ease up when you're talking to people or if you get tired. And you can take the mask off in front of people. Just be sure to check your mouth in a mirror every now and then so you can learn how much effort you need to keep it naturally firm, and then work toward constantly maintaining that state. When you can do it without thinking, your training will be over."

"Wow, really? Okay, then!"

I was making progress, and I was determined to keep it up.

"…That's it from me. Do you have any other concerns?"

"Well…the thing with Natsubaya—I mean Tama-chan… It was like… The way she was acting…"

"…Oh, that," Hinami said. Something was bothering her.

"If it's hard to talk about, you don't have t—"

Hinami interrupted me. "She's very stubborn. Or…sincere, maybe." She still looked troubled. "She doesn't adjust her actions based on the mood around her. She just does what she wants."

"Huh… That's unusual for kids our age, right?"

"Yeah. Her good friends like that about her, myself included. But she doesn't get along with some people."

The game started, and right away I was surprised. I had thought NO NAME was copying my playstyle, but their opening moves showed me I was completely wrong.

I charged at my enemy, already planning my combo. But NO NAME was standing on alert, charging a projectile attack.

It was the one thing I felt could put me at a disadvantage in a mirror match between two Founds.

What's more, it wasn't a coincidence. I didn't have any evidence, but the thought occurred to me all the same.

For some reason, I could tell they'd studied me but weren't merely copying my style. They'd gone as far as developing their own counterstrategy.

Even more surprising was the unparalleled precision of NO NAME's movements and their overwhelming ability to get out of combos. The tiniest hesitation on my part and they were instantly free.

I still had the better neutral game, and I was better at pulling off flashy combos, but honestly speaking, just in terms of escaping, they were already beyond me.

I should admit I'm not very good at that. The reason being I'm too good to get caught very often. It's one of my few weak points.

Basically, don't get comboed to start with, and you'll never need to break out.

That's my approach for all of my moves. Which means the moment NO NAME reaches my level in terms of neutral game and combo potential, I'll lose because I'm not great at escaping.

And I'd be willing to bet NO NAME is already aiming for that goal.

How do I know? It's easy.

Given NO NAME's overall skill level, they're way too good at getting out of combos.

Someone who's this good at the game wouldn't get pulled into combos often enough to practice getting out of them. That's why most of the top players—myself included—are great at offense and not so great at defense.

But this NO NAME...they've got way too much defensive experience for the number two player in Japan. They must have *made* it their strength.

Which means NO NAME has had a lot of opportunities to get into combos—to be specific, they've made a point of getting caught on a regular basis for the sake of practice.

So NO NAME sacrificed the immediate gratification of winrates and the thrill of playing well in exchange for eventual skill and long-term position. They're prioritizing their ability months from now, even if it means being at a disadvantage in whatever game they're currently playing, letting their winrate drop, and watching their ranking and reputation suffer.

Some people might say they're deliberately dropping in the ranks to show off against weaker players, but they'd be wrong. It's right and proper training.

At the very least, I don't know of any other player who's traded instant gratification for such clear and comprehensive results.

NO NAME. I thought I'd be the top player in Japan forever, but I can't be quite so sure anymore. All I can say is this: If any *Atafami* player in Japan is going to pass me up, it'll be this person.

Those were the thoughts running through my mind as we duked it out at our current skill levels, and I won with two lives to spare.

nanashi: gg

It was time for the usual parting exchange. I was planning to cut out as soon as my opponent offered the default reply…

NO NAME: Do you live in the Kanto area?

Huh? They're asking where I live? What are they up to?

nanashi: Yeah…?
NO NAME: Would you like to meet up?
nanashi: You mean irl?
NO NAME: Yes. If it's okay, I'd like to talk and have a rematch.

*   *   *

An invitation to meet offline. Probably one-on-one. *Am I reading this right?*

What should I do? True, it's getting easier to meet face-to-face with people from the Internet these days, and honestly, it's not that dangerous. Given we're already connected by our status as the top two *Atafami* players, meeting up could be interesting. So...

nanashi: Okay, let's do it.

NO NAME: Thank you! What's the closest train station to your house? I was the one who initiated, so I'll come to you.

nanashi: Oh, okay, it's...

I gave the name of a station, and we made plans to meet. It wasn't actually the closest one to my house, but the major terminal a stop over. I figured that would be more convenient for them.

NO NAME: Got it! So I'll see you next Saturday at 2:00. Looking forward to it!

And thus, right after our long-awaited match, NO NAME and I agreed to meet offline like it was no big deal at all.

* * *

After playing Nakamura on Saturday and NO NAME on Sunday, Monday's homeroom in second-year Class 2 was more ordinary than I'd expected. I'd been prepared to find that my place in the pecking order had plunged even further thanks to Nakamura, so I felt a little deflated, but mostly relieved.

Nakamura had a reputation as the best player back in junior high (and thus probably in high school, too), and I was known for my unusual skills, but the match between us hadn't exactly been earthshaking news. Still, word had filtered through the class that it would be the most interesting thing to happen for a couple of weeks. I figured the reason no one was mentioning it now despite the buildup was that they guessed what had happened and were treading lightly around the sore spot. Well, that was the most peaceful outcome I could have hoped for.

My days as a loner passed as they always did. Nothing exciting happened, but I wasn't particularly unhappy. As the saying goes, "If it ain't broke, don't fix it." This was my life, and I was fine with it.

That was the general situation until a minor event occurred on Wednesday afternoon.

I was walking down the hallway on my way to eat lunch by myself, as always, when I ran into Nakamura. Under normal circumstances, we'd have ignored each other, but this time something was different. Nakamura had a girl with him: Aoi Hinami.

Aoi Hinami was the ideal Japanese girl—beautiful and talented, but a little innocent, too. The inarguably perfect heroine, popular with guys and girls alike. Of course, she was at the top of our class academically, but she was also way better than any other girl at sprints and throwing and the rest of PE activities. And not just girls—she was neck and neck with the top guys, too, like some kind of game-breaking character. She wore pleasant, natural makeup and had a friendly smile, and there was something about her that was impossible to hate. I'm not sure whether to call her simple-minded or sincere or just kind of a ditz, but that minor weakness crossed the final *t* on her perfect-girl identity. Admittedly, her charm was a little sexy, too. It's beyond me how she made it all work. I'm terrible at real life, and even I couldn't help liking her. Or maybe I should say I was in awe of her.

I have no idea what she's doing at Sekitomo High School. This may be one of the better private schools in Saitama Prefecture, but it's still Saitama, and compared to the college prep schools in Tokyo, we're average at best. Plus, we're out in the middle of a bunch of rice fields. Get a couple kilometers from a train station in Saitama, and you'll generally find yourself in the middle of nowhere.

I remember overhearing a conversation in class once, when I was sitting behind two other kids. They weren't exactly cool or uncool, but they were definitely cooler than me.

"So what do you think about Aoi-chan?" one of them had asked.

"You mean Aoi Hinami?" the other one said.

"Yeah."

"What do I think? I mean, she's awesome. Doesn't everyone think that? She's a superstar."

"Yeah."

"She's, like, a prodigy. School, sports, looks…everything about her is perfect. 'Genius' still feels like an understatement."

"True that. I know I could never beat her at anything. Neither could you."

"But she still gets along really well with everyone; that's the weird part. If you asked me which girl I got along best with, I'd say Aoi Hinami."

"…Me too. I'm closer to her than any of the others."

"Right? It's strange. She doesn't get anything out of being friends with us, but she doesn't pick and choose. She doesn't use people, I don't think."

"What is it, then? I guess we could call her a genius at life…"

"That's the perfect way of putting it. She's not a baseball genius or a genius inventor or whatever—she's a genius at life. A goddess."

"I wish I could thank her parents for putting her in school here."

"Right? The only thing better about Saitama than Tokyo is that we've got Aoi Hinami."

As I listened to their conversation, I thought, *What's that say about me, then? I can't even make friends with Aoi Hinami—I've never even talked to her! Maybe I'm my own kind of genius.*

I was also thinking they should stop talking about Tokyo all the time and focus on beating Kanagawa first. Or maybe Chiba. We'd never lose to Chiba.

Anyway, Aoi Hinami was there in the hall with Nakamura. Of course, she would have known that Nakamura and I were going to play each other, and that knowledge was the gunpowder for our little explosion.

*"Oh, Tomozaki-kun! I heard you played Shuji in *Atafami*! How was that?"*

"Um, uh, hi, Hinami-san, uh, it was grape."

I was a stuttering mess. I even said *grape* instead of *great*. I'm not going to blame my status as a super-geek; I bet even a casual geek would have stuttered with Aoi Hinami.

"Ha-ha-ha, 'grape'? What are you talking about?!"

She was obviously laughing at me, but weirdly enough, I didn't feel like I was being made fun of. Maybe it was the innocence in her smile, or the beautiful sound of her laugh, or maybe it was how gracefully she covered her mouth with her hand. All I felt was happiness at having made Aoi Hinami-san laugh. What the heck was going on? Her smile was bewitched or something.

"Ha-ha-ha, I enjoyed that! Oh yeah, I almost forgot to ask! Who won?"

Enjoyed it? She enjoyed it! Could there be anything more wonderful than Aoi Hinami-san enjoying something I did?

She was like some kind of saint with the power to put these thoughts in my head. What *was* this?

"Uh, um…"

"Yeah?"

But Nakamura was right there next to us. The sight of me had obviously put him in a bad mood. I couldn't do much about it, though. I'd dug my own grave with that overzealous speech after we played.

The problem was, I didn't know what would happen if I said I won when he was already irritated, and especially when he standing next to the school heroine. He probably wanted to impress her, and he probably wouldn't be too happy if I stole even more of his thunder. Yup, this could get nasty.

Okay, I'll admit, part of me wanted to show off in front of the most popular girl in school. I may be messed up, but I'm still human. On the other hand, I knew it wouldn't lead to anything. In fact, people might be like, *He's too good, what a freak, LOL!* Why? Because life is an unfair, shitty game.

And in that case, it would be better to just smooth things over and say I lost. *Then again, I might end up hurting Nakamura's pride…* And that was when I realized something.

Wait a second. Why was Aoi Hinami, the perfect superwoman, asking *me* this question? Since she was friends with Nakamura, asking him would have been more natural. Was she making conversation to put me at ease because we'd never really talked before? No, someone as attuned to the social climate as Aoi Hinami would have already figured out that Nakamura had lost from the general atmosphere at school lately. Given that, bringing it up with me as a topic of conversation would be an odd move. What was going on?

…I couldn't come up with anything. As I considered how to answer, Nakamura suddenly spoke up.

"God, Aoi, just shut up. I lost, okay? Let's get going and forget about this dweeb," he spat in the most irritated tone I'd ever heard.

The air between us froze. *Uh-oh, now what?*

"Wow! Really? Tomozaki-kun, that's amazing! Come on, Shuji, don't you worry!"

She said "don't you worry" very affectionately, even a little teasingly. The tension softened.

"…Aw, shut up!" he retorted, this time smiling with exasperation.

"But Shuji's good at everything! Wow, you must be super-good if you beat him! That's amazing…"

"N-no, it wasn't a big deal…"

"I want to play you next!"

"I—I don't think that's a very good idea…"

"Yeah, maybe not. Sorry, just got carried away!" She giggled.

For some reason, she was really easy to talk to. I guess this is what people mean when they talk about "communication skills." And Nakamura was standing next to her with this tiny smile, like he was watching over a child, even though she'd just made him admit he'd lost. It must have been the way she teased him a little afterward that did it. If that was the case, she really was amazing.

"Uh, well, I'm off to the cafeteria."

"Okay! See you later. Teach me some of your tricks next time!"

"Uh, yeah."

"…ing…" Nakamura was muttering something.

"What?"

"Nothing. Bye."

What just happened? "Uh, bye."

"Bye!"

I walked off toward the dining hall while Aoi Hinami's second "bye" reached the back of my head.

…*Whew. I survived.* I let out a sigh of relief.

But now it was all starting to make sense. She must have known from the start that even if she brought up that topic, she'd be able to get everyone feeling okay, even excited, by the end of the conversation. A decision only a normie could make. There was no way my brain could have predicted it.

All the same, I hadn't expected Nakamura to reveal that he'd lost. *Hopefully that won't make him hate me even more…* With that thought on my mind, I arrived at the dining hall.

That's how the little explosion in my everyday life was softened by the formidable communication skills of Aoi Hanami before it shrank and faded away. I normally can't stand the weird confidence and excessive enthusiasm of normies, and I used to think it didn't serve any purpose. But I had to admit, Aoi Hanami was incredible. My values had shifted a little, marking a small milestone in my life.

The following Saturday, a much bigger event occurred.

"I'm here!"

"I'll be there in two minutes."

"Okay!"

The day of my meeting with NO NAME had arrived. I'd gotten a message saying, *"If you need to contact me, use this e-mail address!"* so now we were e-mailing. It seemed NO NAME was already waiting. I took the train one stop and arrived as well.

"I'm here."

"Okay! I'm waiting outside the convenience store by the east exit."

"Got it. What are you wearing?"

I could see the convenience store right across from the east exit. There was an ashtray outside with a couple of guys standing around it, smoking. *Which one is NO NAME?*

My cell phone vibrated. I opened the message. Okay, then.

"I'm wearing a white and blue shirt and a black skirt!"

A girl. Well, I guess that's possible. I assumed it was a guy, but there's no reason for it not to be a girl.

I walked over to the convenience store and looked around until I spotted a girl in front of the vending machine. White and blue shirt, and a black skirt. It was her.

From the back, I could see she had silky black shoulder-length hair and skin so fair it was nearly transparent. I couldn't see her face, but she was probably young. Even from behind, I could tell she was cute. *Oh shit. Now I'm nervous about saying hi. Hope my voice doesn't crack.*

"Uh, 'scuse me, are you NO NAME?"

I managed to say it okay. The pure and innocent black-haired girl started to turn toward me. What would she look—*huh?*

"Hi! Yes, I'm NO NAME...huh?"

"...Uh...? ...Err..."

"Ehhhhhh?!"

Before I could even express my surprise, Aoi Hinami screamed.

Aoi Hinami?! What's going on?

"Um...Hinami...san?"

"Okay, give me a sec. I need to calm down... You're definitely Tomozaki-kun, right? From my class?"

"Uh, um, yeah..."

This was no Aoi Hinami look-alike. It was the real deal. But what hit me before the surprise was her strange behavior. She sounded totally different from usual. Like, not at all cheerful. Cold. At the same time, though, it didn't feel like an act.

"*You're* nanashi?" Her tone was kind of aggressive.

"Yeah, that's me…," I answered awkwardly.

"…!"

A sharp crease appeared between her eyebrows. *Huh?* The Aoi Hanami I knew didn't scowl like that. She was more innocent, daintier…

"Well, this sucks…"

"Huh?"

"I don't want to believe this. I don't want to believe the real nanashi is a loser who's going nowhere in life."

"H-Hinami-san?"

What did she just say? "A loser who's going nowhere in life"? She wasn't the type to insult a guy right to his face, was she? What's going on? Does she have a split personality? Or was I too much of a freak even for her?

"Wh-what's wrong? Hinami-san, you're not…yourself. The way you're talking and stuff."

"!"

She leaned way back, looking extremely uncomfortable. Her face is very expressive, so it was easy to read her mood. Normally, she uses that quality to a much cuter effect, of course.

"Oh… I've got to stop forgetting myself when it comes to *Atafami*…"

"Huh?"

"But if that's all you saw, it's whatever."

"Whatever…?"

"You said I'm just talking and acting weird, right? If that's all you noticed, then it's not a problem."

"Not a problem…?"

Um, yes it is. It's a huge problem. Who are you and what have you done with Hinami-san?!

"…"

"…"

An unexpected silence descended over us. *Well, this is awkward.* But Aoi Hinami just stood there with that intimidating frown on her face, making no effort whatsoever to ease the tension.

"W-well anyway, so you're NO NAME. That's a surprise…I mean…"

I even stumbled over finding a couple of words to fill the silence. Well, at least I'm consistent.

"Yup. I'm disappointed, too. I can't believe that nanashi, the one person I respected, turned out to be garbage without the slightest spark of ambition. You're the type who's willing to just give up and lose at life."

"…Huh?"

I was already busy beating myself up, and here comes the outside world to give me another kick when I'm down. She was being really harsh. I mean, "garbage"? She did say something about respect, but that was in the past tense. I'd been preoccupied by how different she was from her school self, but I couldn't let her diss me this badly without saying something.

"W-wait a second. Um, was all that…necessary?"

"I only said it 'cause it's true."

"Just because it's true…doesn't mean it's okay to say it."

"What's that supposed to mean?"

"You don't even know me, and you're saying I d-don't have any ambition and that I just let myself be a loser… What I'm trying to say is, you don't have any right to lecture me. I think it's rude."

"Maybe you should stop talking with your mouth full before you start telling people not to be rude, don't you think?"

"I don't have anything in my mouth!"

I opened my mouth wide and finally managed to talk without stuttering. Aoi Hinami eyed me coldly.

"…Okay, I'll give you that. I guess I was rude. I owe you an apology. I'm sorry. When it comes to that game, I get kind of worked up… But I'm gonna to tell you something, and I'm giving you fair warning it's rude… I'm upset because the only person I respected turns out to be the type of person I hate most."

"That's what I'm talking about…"

"You have no right to talk about manners. Look at what you're wearing."

Huh? What do my clothes have to do with anything? It's not like there's a dress code.

"Wh-what do you mean? People can wear whatever they want."

"…Hmph. That's exactly why I hate your type."

"Huh?"

She was still going. Even though she had apologized two seconds ago.

"When you meet someone, especially for the first time, there's a minimum standard for what to wear, right? Okay, I know we technically aren't meeting for the first time, but you didn't know that, did you? Look at the wrinkles in your shirt. Did you even bother to iron it? And the cuffs of your jeans are all raggedy. How long have you had those? Have you considered buying a new pair? It's been ages since I saw a high school student wearing high-tech sneakers. They're all muddy, and the laces are frayed. It's obvious you walked over here with them untied. And come on—your hair looks like you just rolled out of bed. Did you brush it at all this morning? Did you even look in a mirror? If you were meeting someone for the first time, and they showed up looking like you do now, wouldn't you think they were rude? Well, Tomozaki-kun?"

After her tirade, I was suddenly aware of my appearance. I hadn't thought about it earlier, but I suppose you could say I wasn't dressed very well. Okay, so she was right about *one* thing. Still, what's her problem? I didn't come here to get roasted by someone I barely knew.

"B-but it's none of your business, is it? It's a free country."

"Yes, it is. If that's good enough for you, I guess that's fine. It's just that you said I was rude, but you're just as bad. That's all I wanted to say."

"Just as bad?"

"Well, this isn't actually the first time we've met, so you don't have to apologize. If this really was the first time, then you should have, though."

The expression in her eyes was worse than contempt for literal garbage and more in the realm of actual hatred.

"…But now I've said enough that I really am being rude. I don't think any of it was wrong, but I'll apologize again. For being rude, that is. I'm sorry. I don't feel like talking about *Atafami* or having a rematch anymore. Good-bye."

With that, Aoi Hinami turned on her heels and started walking toward the station. I caught a glimpse of her face as she went.

*   *   *

I'm not sure myself of the reason I went and opened my mouth. I should have been more than happy to say good-bye to someone so rude. Maybe I was annoyed about what she'd said, or maybe it was because for that brief moment when she turned away, she looked more dejected than hateful.

"…Wait. You think you can say whatever you want and then leave?"

Aoi Hinami stopped and looked back at me. "*Sigh*. Now what do you want?"

I'd been running my mouth to stop her, so to be honest, I didn't have a follow-up. I was too worked up to read her expression very well, but behind the hatred I thought I saw a glimmer of hope at the same time. My mind was a blank. I was only conscious of a growing chill in my fingertips.

"You said I was losing at life or something."

I didn't know what I was going to say next. My heartbeat reverberated in my lungs and rattled my brain.

"You've got great base stats, so someone like you wouldn't get how I feel."

Aoi Hinami's mouth moved ever so slightly, like she was repeating my words, but I couldn't hear her. I wasn't even sure what my voice sounded like just then.

"Life is unfair. I'm ugly, I have a bad build, I overthink until I can't do anything, I'm wishy-washy, people make fun of everything I do, and I have no confidence in my ability to communicate. How is someone like me supposed to beat someone strong like you?"

This might have been the first time I ever said something like that to a stranger.

"But that's all fine. Because life's not fair. You don't get results just by trying hard. If you could, I would, but life doesn't have rules. No rewards, no right answers. As a game, it's a piece of shit. If there's no right answer, then there's no point in trying. And I hate the way normies like you live. Your confidence is totally baseless, and you go around in packs just pretending to have fun."

With the floodgates opened, I couldn't stop myself.

"Even when I have a reason to be confident, I shy away. When I'm in a group I just feel alone, and it's not fun. I'm used to this life. I don't know why things are this way. You have a problem with that? I've been like this as long as I can remember. That's fine with me. I'm a loner, but I have my fun. I'm fine with this..."

I clenched my fists.

"...So don't force your values on me!"

I felt the heat suddenly drain away. The thick mist cleared from my head, the fire in my eyes began to dim, and Aoi Hinami's expression gradually came into focus.

Her face was blank. She was just staring at me.

"...Stop crying like a sore loser," she mumbled matter-of-factly.

"What?"

"I said, you're a sore loser. You hate the way 'normies' live when you've never experienced it yourself? That's idiotic. How do you know you hate it? If you'd experienced it and then said it wasn't any fun, that would make sense. But you've never experienced it, have you? In that case you're just a sore loser."

...I had the feeling I'd heard a similar argument in the past. The very recent past.

"There's nothing I hate more than someone who loses and starts trying to justify the loss instead of making an effort to improve."

That argument really did sound familiar.

But this wasn't the same thing.

"I get what you're saying, but this is different. You can't change characters in real life."

"Characters?"

"The moment we're born, our futures are pretty much decided. You're good-looking and good at academics and sports. You're top-tier. If I was like you, I'd be doing a little better in life. But I'm not. All my skill points went into things like hair-splitting and a tendency to be contrarian. It doesn't help in life at all; it actually makes me think too much until I lose all confidence and motivation. What do you expect? My hands are tied!"

Aoi Hinami was eyeing me silently, so I kept talking.

"Your character is just better than mine. And that's fine. I've honestly enjoyed my life just like it is. So leave me the hell alone..."

"A better character, huh?"

Aoi Hinami glanced down and to the side for a moment. Then suddenly, she spoke again.

"Come with me." She grabbed my arm.

"Huh?"

With that, I was dragged away, dumbfounded and not entirely willing, by Aoi Hinami.

* * *

So there I was, sitting with my legs politely folded under me (but still slouching) as I scanned the room searching for the source of a very sweet smell for lack of anything better to do. I didn't see any perfume or incense. But the smell was so sweet and pleasant that it had to be coming from somewhere.

There was a bed with white sheets and a light-yellow terrycloth blanket. A pink pillow and a pair of soft, clearly well-loved pajamas on top. A little black oval table with nothing on it except a cutesy orange pen and a black lamp. A white dresser and bookcase. A stylish black desk. Pale pink carpeting. The only other things in the room were a couple of simple, warm-colored knickknacks that were vaguely cute and tidy-looking. She hadn't had time to spray an air freshener or anything like that.

Maybe the fabric?

I could be convinced that the room had taken on the smell of her clothes, sheets, blanket, and carpet. But to achieve that, she would really have to be on top of cleaning and laundry and stuff. If I hadn't seen the completely transformed Aoi Hinami of a little while ago, I'd have believed the perfect heroine was capable of this, but not anymore.

What was her problem anyway? She just said whatever the hell she wanted and made me say things I didn't want to say. Usually, if you dragged a boy from your class who you hardly knew into your room against his will, that would be considered insanely ru... *Wait a second, I'm in Aoi Hinami's room!*

I'd been vaguely aware of what was happening and tried to ignore it, but in truth, I was in deep trouble. I'd never been in a girl's room before, and I had no idea what I was supposed to do. For the moment, I was just sitting on the floor. I'd probably already done ten things wrong.

The girl in question had left me there by myself, muttering a very mysterious "A better character, huh?" on her way out. She'd only been gone a few minutes, but I could already feel my mind trying to strangle me from the inside.

I'd managed to trick myself into staying calm by thinking about a variety of other topics, but I was about to break. *Give me some peace already!*

Thump, thump, thump. Someone was climbing the stairs, so this room must be on the second floor. I was panicking so badly I had *actually* forgotten I was on the second floor. Was Aoi Hinami back?

Click. The door to the room opened.

"...Uh, I'm just visiting."

A girl I'd never seen before came in. Even I have enough communication skills—or should I say manners—to offer a proper greeting in this situation. Honestly, she wasn't as pretty as Aoi Hinami, although there was a slight resemblance. Probably her older sister or something. I bet she was wondering why that perfect beautiful girl had let this dud into her room. I just hoped she didn't feel the need to say so out loud.

"What do you think?" she said.

"About what?"

"A C-plus, maybe?"

"What's a C-plus?"

"...You really have no experience with girls, do you?"

"Huh...?"

I didn't even know her. What did I do to deserve that? The knack for sudden rude comments to super-geeks must run in the blood of the Hinami family.

"I'm not wearing makeup."

"What?"

"It's me, Aoi Hinami. I took off my makeup. How dumb are you?"

"...Ehhhh—?!"

I did notice a resemblance, but still, how could she look this different? I never got the impression she wore super-heavy makeup. In fact, it was the opposite—I thought she was the natural type. What was going on?

"You said my character was better than yours, right?"

"...? Yeah, and...?"

"Do you understand now?"

"...Understand what?"

"You're so dumb, it's almost criminal. Obviously, I mean that with a little effort, your appearance parameter can improve."

"Oh."

So that's what she meant. I got what she was saying, but that still didn't give her the right to lecture me.

"Even if you're a low-tier character, you can improve yourself. Your face's base stats aren't an excuse for giving up on life."

You sure about that?

"...That's it? You brought me up here to lecture me with clichés?"

"Pretty much."

"It's really none of your business. I already told you, we're different. First of all, I'm a guy, so I can't wear makeup. Plus, our initial status is different. My facial structure is what it is. What can I do about it now? That's just part of being bottom-tier... Anyway, I'm going home."

I picked up my bag and stood up, less tense than before. Maybe because I'd just vented everything that was on my mind.

"You really don't get it at all."

"...What now?"

"What do you think the most important elements of a person's appearance are? Tell me three."

"I said I was leaving. Do I still have to play your little game?"

"Oh, so life isn't the only thing you run from. You aren't even up for a tiny little fight. You really are a sore loser."

The insults kept coming. She had some nerve.

"Give it a rest already! Fine, if you insist, I'll take your bait. Important elements of a person's appearance. The face they're born with, for one. What else? Their height and weight, I guess."

"Wrong."

Shot down.

"Okay, then what?"

"Your facial expression, build, and posture."

I basically said build, didn't I? "…What about your face itself?"

"Not a major issue."

"Uh, I doubt that…"

How could your face not matter to your overall appearance? Obviously it did. My own life was proof.

"Then have a look at this."

Aoi Hinami covered her face with both hands. She straightened up, then took her hands away like she was playing peek-a-boo. "How's this for you?"

"…Uh, what just happened…?"

The girl in front of me was surprisingly pretty, as well as 50 or 60 percent friendlier-looking than before she hid her face. She looked like Aoi Hinami without her makeup on. Actually, shouldn't she have looked like this before?

"Do you get it now? It's all in my expression."

"No way… It's gotta be more than that."

"So how do you explain it? Some kind of quick-change magic trick? Instant plastic surgery?" As she spoke, she let the energy drain from her face until it was what she had called a "C-plus" again. But even as that thought entered my mind, she was changing back to the friendly beauty. Again and again, she flipped back and forth.

"Oooh…"

I felt like I was watching an amazing skill. It was really impressive, honestly.

"Okay, I admit I had to practice a lot to get this good," she said, slowly transforming once again. "By the way, did you notice that I'm changing my posture as well as my expression?"

"Huh?"

Now that she mentioned it, if I watched closely, I could see her back hunching over as the energy drained from her face, then straightening again as she became more genial and attractive.

"Your posture affects the impact of your facial expression. Just by perfecting your expression and posture, you'll be more than able to convince people you're a normie. Of course, I was blessed with a nice face to begin with, which is why I can get *this* beautiful."

"You're a confident one, aren't you, Your Highness?"

"Exactly. Confidence is key."

"That's not what I meant! …Anyway, what's your point?"

"You don't know?"

…*Okay, I guess I do.*

"You're trying to say that even an ugly bastard can manage to look ordinary, at least?"

"Ooh, you *are* good at guessing!"

"So what? You want me to try harder? Didn't I already tell you it's none of your business?"

"It's not that."

"What, then?"

Aoi Hinami looked me in the eye—or more accurately, she gazed so deeply into my pupils it was like she could see into my brain.

"It's that people like you, or at least, this version of you, have the most despicable souls of anyone in the whole world."

"Wha—?" *What the hell are you suddenly attacking me for?*

"I did say 'this version of you.'"

"Th-this version? …Don't think you can distract me by trying to imply—"

"You're about to get a very smug lecture, but don't feel obligated to pay attention. I do plan to give you orders, but ultimately, you're the one who'll decide whether or not to obey them. You're free to ignore everything I say. Keep that in mind."

Aoi Hinami cut me off, changing the mood. There wasn't a shred of humor in her words or eyes. Even someone as socially awkward and oblivious as me could tell this was as serious as she got.

"...Uh-huh..." Her quiet drive and composure, way beyond what you'd expect from a normal high school girl, overwhelmed me.

Having gotten my consent, she began to explain. Her expression was neither the lackluster C-plus face nor the friendly, pretty one, but instead something sorrowful and very human.

"...You said you don't have communication skills or confidence, and compared to you, my base stats are high. But they're not. To be honest, I was an average person—below average, even, at least through elementary school. That's why I'm not beating around the bush. Communication skills and confidence and the other things you mentioned—all of those can improve with effort. My life since junior high is proof."

Her confident tone suggested that her claims were well-supported.

"...You said life was irrational and unfair, but that's not true. The game of life functions on a number of simple rules. You just can't see them because they intersect in complex ways."

I could tell she was getting in my head, whether I believed her or not.

"I respected nanashi. I've gotten through a lot with effort alone. I was confident that I was better than anyone when it came to hard work and perseverance, and the results would show that. But I just couldn't reach nanashi's level in *Atafami*."

Her explanation continued. She didn't move or gesture hardly at all.

"I thought nanashi could outdo me in effort, and that's why I respected him. But behind the curtain, this is what I found. When it came to real life, nanashi not only lost, he didn't even put up a fight. Then, he was a worthless deadbeat who used his default attributes as an excuse to run away. Worst of all, he was a pathetic sore loser trying to justify himself by jumping to the conclusion that a pleasure he'd never experienced must be boring."

Strangely, despite everything she was saying about me, I didn't feel angry. Maybe I was overwhelmed by her earnestness and intensity, but more than that, I was starting to sense a similarity between us.

"I'm an amazing person. You think so too, don't you? I might even be the most amazing sixteen-year-old in Japan. But in one area, you're beating me. We're the same age, and gender doesn't matter for this. So I'm going to go ahead and say it: It makes me sick to know that you, the person who's beating me—nanashi, the one person I respected—is ruining his life. It's unforgivable! It's disgusting! If the person beating me is worthless, doesn't that make me worthless, too?"

I think the reason she didn't strike me as arrogant even after everything she'd said was that she had obviously paid in blood and sweat for all her success.

"It's my pet theory that the best games are always the simplest. The game of life looks like it doesn't have any rules, but actually, it's just an elegant, complex intersection of the simplest rules. You said life's a shitty game, but that's ridiculous. There's no better game in the world. You just don't know it yet… Nanashi is a great gamer, so how can I let him keep losing at such a wonderful game? …Tomozaki-kun, I'm going to give you an offer—no, an order."

Details aside, I'd never met someone whose basic worldview was so close to my own. That's exactly why—

"I'm going to teach you the rules of this game one by one."

—her explanation made so much sense it was almost annoying.

"It's time for you to get serious about playing the game of life!"

That was the major event that took place on Saturday.

* * *

"Okay, I get what you're trying to say."

I don't think I'd ever been lectured this honestly and with so little BS by a person I hardly knew.

"Good." Aoi Hinami's face was still her real one, far as I could tell.

"But there are a few things I still don't understand." Yes or no, I couldn't afford to give a perfunctory answer to a question like this.

"I think the game of life is trash. I can back that up with a lot of proof, and I'm fairly confident I'm right."

The bottom tier gets exploited, and the top tier reaps the benefits. There are no simple, elegant rules. It's just a shitty game.

"Yes..."

"So when you say life's a great game, and that I'm just making excuses, and I'm a sore loser, it doesn't sit right with me."

"Right."

"But..."

"But?"

As I spoke, I remembered how Nakamura blamed his loss on the game itself. "I agree with you. Not making any effort and covering up your loss by blaming it on the game is the most pathetic thing in the world. There's nothing I hate more."

Aoi Hinami's mouth stretched into a wide smile.

"Really? Now that's worthy of nanashi."

"...But sometimes it really is the game's fault. In many games, you can make up for a shitty character with technique, but there are a few where it's just impossible."

"And you want to say life is one of those games where it's just impossible, right?"

"Right. That's why it's garbage."

"In your view."

"Maybe. But I don't know how to look at life the way you do."

"Of course you don't."

"Yeah, obviously. People can't see through someone else's eyes. In a game, you can try out a top-tier character, but in real life, you can't try on another person's perspective. My only choice is to trust my own view of things."

"Uh-huh..."

"So when someone says life is the G.O.A.T. or whatever, I figure it's just because they're a top-tier character. Their opinion isn't gonna change my mind." I looked Aoi Hinami straight in the eye. "And that's my perspective."

This time, the disappointment on her face was clear.

"…Yeah. That's fine, then. The final decision is yo—"

"But," I interrupted. "…But this time, I'm starting to think it might be worth it to hear you out a little longer."

Again, I looked her straight in the eye. *Damn. She really is attractive.*

"Why do you say that?"

"Because…" I thought for a moment. "Because the way you put it is too similar to mine, even if you are a normie with good looks. I think we have enough in common that I might learn something from you."

"Hmm."

"But that's not the main reason."

"…And what would that be?"

Her gaze shifted toward me with interest and suspicion.

"The person who's saying this stuff is the only gamer in Japan I respect—NO NAME."

"…"

"…"

"…Lame."

Huh? I thought I nailed it!

"…Wait, how was that lame?"

"You can't just slap on a weird one-liner at the end. It's lame."

"Cut me some slack; it took all my courage to say that."

"Don't care. You might think it was deep, but it wasn't."

"Hey, I have problems with communication. How 'bout an A for effort, at least? I respond well to praise."

"Did you do something praiseworthy? No, you disappointed me. Nan-ashi would never change his mind that easily."

"Huh? What was easy about it? And I didn't change my mind; I just said I was willing to hear you out a little longer."

"How's that any different? Sounds the same to me."

"No way. I trust gamers, and you're the second best in Japan. That means the person I trust more than anyone, other than myself, is saying there's something I don't know. Which is why I'll listen. That's all."

"Doesn't that mean you changed your mind?"

"I already told you, no! I'm just gonna listen and then decide if you've convinced me. I'm a long way from accepting your offer. If you don't convince me, no dice."

"But you'll listen to me for now."

"Of course. I'm nanashi. It only took one game for me to tell how much effort you put into honing your skills. I think listening to you will be worth my while."

"…Hmph…I guess."

"I guess," huh?

I was about to congratulate myself on surviving a whole conversation with a classmate, and a heated one at that…when I realized I wasn't actually talking to Aoi Hinami. I was talking to NO NAME. Maybe it wasn't that impressive after all.

"Well, teach me already. What are the rules?"

I wanted to judge for myself whether the game of life was as "god-tier" as they say.

"Tomozaki-kun, you really don't get it. I already told you, the rules intersect in complex ways. They're not that easy to teach."

"You can't teach me? What the hell? Why did you change your tune all of a sudden?"

"…Okay, consider this. When you buy a new game and bring it home, do you get good by reading the instruction manual?"

"What's that got to do with it?"

"Just answer the question."

"…No. I mean, I do read the instructions, but to get good you have to play. Otherwise, you won't understand what it's really about."

"Exactly. They're the same."

"The same?"

"You don't master games by reading the instruction manual. Same with real life."

Same with real life? I thought about that for a second, but before I could answer, Hinami started talking again.

"You usually try playing new games without reading much of the instructions, right?"

I nodded.

"Life's the same. You won't get good without playing."

…That didn't sound right. After all, I'd been playing all my life.

"Wait a second. The reason I'm the way I am is because I've been failing this whole time."

"Exactly. And when you're having trouble in a game, what do you do?"

"In a game? Well, it depends what kind…but I might level up, practice, look at some strategy websites… That's about it…"

"Spoken like nanashi himself. Correct."

"And?"

"You can do all those in life, too. That's the essence of the game." She grinned.

"…Wait a second— No, I do get what you're saying. You're telling me to level up—to make an effort? I guess that's the only option."

"Right."

"But it doesn't work as well in real life as in other games. You can try till you're blue in the face—it won't make a difference. The limits are set when you start it up, and you can't undo them. It's a shitty setup in any game, including life. But you probably wouldn't understand… After all, you're a top-tier character."

"Do you really understand?"

"Understand what?"

"Leveling up means self-improvement. It's the work of increasing your basic abilities, from your appearance to your inner attributes. Practicing means improving the skills you need for getting ahead in the world—in other words, polishing the more concrete and practical abilities. Do those two things, and you'll clear most of what life throws at you."

"…Okay, I do get what you're trying to say, but it's not that easy. When you're at the bottom like me, there are tons of impossible problems when it comes to leveling up or practicing."

"Uh-huh. Leaving aside the question of whether you've ever even tried, I'll admit, sometimes that's true."

"So you do admit it? Then I'm doomed?"

"Those seemingly impossible problems are what we could call life's 'hard stages,' and there are ways to deal with those. You already said it. Leveling up, practicing...and one more."

That would be...

"Oh."

"Yeah. Strategy sites."

"...What's a strategy site in real life, then? Self-improvement books or how-to books? You're saying I can figure it out just by reading some of those?"

"Oh dear," Hinami said, giggling. "Well, I suppose that would work, too. But there's only one strategy site in the world that's one hundred percent guaranteed to work if you just follow what it says."

"What are you talking about? That's too convenient; no way."

"It's real. Although, I only know of one."

"...So what is it already? Where would I find it?"

"Well...," Hinami said, tapping her head slowly two times with her pointer finger.

"Right here."

Her tone was playful and her expression overflowing with confidence. She might as well have been saying, "Obviously!"

"...I've got nothin'. Your confidence is something else."

I couldn't help but laugh. It was surprisingly refreshing to take such a clean hit.

"Naturally. I've had to beat the game out of necessity so far. I've drilled every cause-effect relationship into my head."

It kinda made sense, but kinda didn't.

"Cause and effect, huh? ...Are those the rules for life you're talking about?"

"Exactly."

"Hmm..."

The rule for the life I know is that top-tier players get the benefits and low-tier players get exploited. Everyone hates contrarians and cowards, and hurting other people makes you look strong. The game of life is garbage because those shitty rules are all there is. But this girl was boasting that life had other rules—rules that could turn it into a great game.

She'd gotten real results, and that was persuasive. Her basic worldview was close to my own, so it was something I could accept. I was starting to think I might as well go for it—to get serious about the game of life.

But no. She was wrong. The more I thought about it, the more it seemed we probably wouldn't ever understand each other. After all, that's how things always end up with this type.

I asked her a question as a test.

"…So let's say life is god-tier, then. Let me ask you this: Where does it fall in relation to the rest of the tier, among other games?"

That's the crux of it. That's the gulf between people who praise the game of life and me.

"How good? …Well, as far as I know…" She looked up, briefly hesitant. "Far and away the best, I'd say."

See that?

That's what I'm talking about. In the end, people who say life's the G.O.A.T. are just looking down on all other games. They pretend to compare life to a game when it's convenient, but in fact they view it as something special and superior. They assume other games are worthless from the start and only throw life in as a comparison after they've turned up their nose at all the others.

And this girl was doing the same thing. Disappointed, I wordlessly took my bag and got ready to stand up.

Just then, she started talking again.

"Actually…now that I think about it, it's tied with *Atafami*."

Her voice was so natural it caught me off guard, and so innocent the revelation was anticlimactic.

"What?"

"Yeah. I was on the fence for a minute, but I decided it's impossible to say which one is better. I mean, ideally I'd be able to say life was better, but…unfortunately, it's a tie."

I was stunned. A tie for first place? Between life and *Atafami*?

Did she really just say that? The ultimate normie, Aoi Hinami?

"Are you disappointed? After all, you've already mastered *Atafami*. It might not be worth your while to try out another game that isn't any more fun."

"...You..."

Disappointed? That's crazy. In spite of myself—

"Yes, that does make sense," Hinami continued, muttering rapidly. "You're already the best at one of the best games...which means I needed to offer you something even more valuable... Damn, I messed up. I always act before I think when it comes to *Atafami*. I really need to get better about that..."

She looked at me again.

"Well, I did say the choice was yours, and it doesn't matter what you decide. It would be wrong to gain your trust by lying, so I guess that's that."

"I..."

I almost spoke my mind but caught myself. Up to this point, I'd been practicing *Atafami* because I wanted to, without anyone knowing. I really wanted to get better, and success made me feel satisfied and happy. It was fun, and that was enough.

But I also realized that I wasn't likely to win anyone's approval for it. The most I would get is some praise on the Internet. I didn't have any gamer friends, my parents never gassed me up for it, and it wouldn't make me popular at school. I'm bad at sports, and I don't have a girlfriend, obviously. Meanwhile, I spent my time on *Atafami* and got results, for me and me alone. That really was enough. I didn't think I needed anyone's approval.

But now this girl—the strongest normie I knew—was saying that life and *Atafami* were in the same tier as games. In other words, she was saying *Atafami* had as much value as life, and she was saying it like an obvious fact.

This from the girl who knew life better than anyone.

Of course, the emotion I felt was contradictory. I'd always thought life was a shitty game. The logical thing would have been for me to argue that *Atafami* was way more fun. *It's the best game there is*, I should've said. *Don't compare it to garbage; quit messing around.*

But now this girl who was better than anyone I knew at life—the most widely accepted game in the real world—was telling me *Atafami* had equal value. I wasn't sure what to think.

I didn't think it mattered if anyone gave my efforts their stamp of approval. Which is good, because no one did. That effort was by me, for me, and I didn't think I minded. I even thought it would be wrong if I *did* mind. But now...

Incredibly enough, I was getting affirmation from someone.

"What's that expression for?"

"...I..." I looked down, trying to hide my feelings.

"Anything with rules is a game, in my opinion. As long as there are rules and results based on those rules, it's all a game."

Aoi Hinami waited quietly for me to continue.

"If that's true of life, then life's a game. If those rules are simple, elegant, and deep, it's one of the best. If not, it's trash... You agree with me there, right?"

"Yes, absolutely. Life has rules, which makes it a proper game. And... because those rules are simple, elegant, and deep, it's a great one."

"...Okay. I understand." I looked up. "In that case..."

"Yes?"

I met Hinami's eyes.

"The gamer in me wants to play."

Surprise colored Hinami's face. I don't know what expression was on my own face when I said that, but it must have been enough to catch her off guard.

"That doesn't mean I trust everything you said, though." I was talking to the gamer in front of me.

"The game is right in front of our eyes. It's a challenging one, but everyone in the whole world is taking part, so there are a lot of players. I'd only played a little before deciding it was shit, but now I've heard from a reliable source that it's actually great. One of the top players is standing here saying she'll teach me some high-level strats. So…"

I ignored the dumbfounded shock on Hinami's face and kept talking.

"There's no reason not to play *the game*."

When I finished talking, I looked up. The stunned Hinami had vanished, and NO NAME was standing in her place with an excited smile.

"…A speech worthy of nanashi."

"What can I say?"

"Do you trust me now?"

"No way. I won't trust you until I play for myself and see if it's really the best."

It was true. I wasn't ready to trust her just yet. Still, like me, she thought like a gamer, and she was giving other games a fair shake when she said life was one of the best. After all, it was as good as *Atafami* according to her. It wouldn't hurt to give it a try.

"But that's how it goes with games. You can't judge until you've played. And if you're gonna play, you've gotta take it seriously from the start or else it's pointless. I don't want to end up making excuses."

"Exactly," Hinami said, nodding and smiling.

"So I'm gonna try it out. I'm gonna play so I can beat the game like a real normie, but I'm not cutting any corners. How's that sound?"

Hinami nodded, as if to say *"Of course!"*

"All right, then. Where do I start?"

"Oh, I like your attitude."

For some reason, she sounded really happy. She stood up, went over to her desk, and started rummaging through it.

"What are you doing?"

"Life is a game that gives you a lot of freedom."

"Huh? Well, okay, but…"

"And when you have a lot of freedom, what do you do first?"

"Um…"

Freedom? Does she mean those games where you can steal a car and go around killing people, or run around naked while robbing stores? If I thought about what they had in common…

"You create your character."

"Hexactly," she said with a straight face, pointing at me.

"Huh? What did you say? *Hex*actly?"

"The first thing you do is create your character."

"No, what did you say before that?"

"…What do you mean? You must be imagining things," she said curtly, looking away.

What was going on? Something about this seemed familiar.

More importantly, why did she say I was imagining things? I started to protest, but she ignored me… *Better just move on.*

"…So character creation?"

"Yes."

Now she looked calm and peaceful, like nothing had happened. I didn't get her. Whatever.

"But my character is already complete… And boy, is he ugly. Ha-ha."

"You give up too easily. Use this."

She ignored my cocky attempt at a joke and pulled something white out of the drawer.

It was… *Just wait a second!*

"…Oh geez. You're not going to suggest I hide behind that all the time, are you?"

"Nope. There's a better way to use it."

In her right hand, she was holding a face mask, the kind people strap over their nose and mouth during allergy season.

* * *

"…I'm back…"

When I got home, I spoke the standard greeting, although not too loud since I was saying it more out of habit than to inform anyone in particular.

I had to pass through the living room to get to my room, and that's when my mom noticed I looked different than usual.

"Fumiya, did you catch a cold?"

"Uh, um, uh-huh."

I hadn't, but I couldn't explain what was going on, so I made vague noises of agreement.

"If you needed a mask, you could have asked. Did you buy that yourself?"

"Uh, no, my friend gave it to me 'cause I said I had a cold."

"Oh really?"

She looked half surprised, half impressed. She didn't have to say it: *Oh, you have a friend close enough to give you a mask for free?* Call it the bond between parent and child.

"Anyway, welcome back. Dinner's almost ready, so go ahead and—"

"I know, I know."

She always says the same thing when I get home. *Take a bath before dinner.* I cut her off mid-sentence and headed off toward the bathroom.

"Oh wait, actually..."

Bang!

"Okay!"

I opened the door on my little sister in her underwear and got so flustered, I answered a question that nobody had asked.

"Eww, you're such a freak, Fumiya."

She ignored me and coolly pulled on her sweatshirt, not looking particularly surprised. It was her fuzzy, oversize black one. Her stretched-out black bra, which was the wrong size for her modest chest, disappeared underneath it.

"I know you're lying."

"Huh?"

As she made her abrupt and cryptic accusation, she turned to me, wearing just her sweatshirt and panties. *How about putting some pants on already?*

"That." She pointed to the lower half of my face.

"The mask?"

"You said your friend gave it to you."

"Uh-huh." *I know where this is going.*

"You don't have any friends who'd give you a face mask."

"Hey..."

This is just one of the annoyances of having a sister one year behind you at the same school.

"You shouldn't tell lies that are so obvious."

She's in her first year, but you'd never guess we were related from her exceedingly good looks and bright personality, which have made her plenty of older friends in my class. Thanks to that, she apparently hears snippets of information about me. *Still, I don't see why I have to listen to my little sister lecture me in the etiquette of lying.*

"Hey, I do too know someone."

After all, I did get the mask from someone, so I wasn't lying.

"Okay, who? Who gave it to you?"

"Why should I tell you?"

"See? You won't tell me, so you must be lying."

Ugh. "Aoi Hinami."

"..."

My sister peered into my face. *I'm not lying, girl. Gotcha!*

For some reason, she sighed.

"What's that for?"

"Listen, that's not a friend." She sounded exasperated. "The reason she gave you a mask is because she's an angel. Get it? She's nice to everyone. It's not about being friends...she's just a really good classmate."

She sounded like she was lecturing a little kid out of pity. Anyway, I didn't think of Aoi Hinami as a friend. If I did, she was more like a war buddy. And an angel? No way. A valkyrie, maybe, but no angel.

"Don't take it the wrong way and fall for her or something. You'll embarrass me."

"You think I'd fall for someone that rude?"

"...Huh? What?"

"Nothing."

"Argh! You're mumbling, and then with that mask on, I can't understand anything you're saying!"

With that, she ripped the mask off my face. Damn.

"...I honestly don't get it. So creepy," she said, pushing grumpily past me... *No wonder.* "I really don't get it," she said again.

In the mirror, this creep had a grin so wide it was almost too big for the mask.

* * *

I looked at the mask in Hinami's hand, confused.

"What do I use that for aside from hiding part of my face? ...Also..."

I was even more confused by where we were than by the mask.

"...Why'd you make me come over here?"

After Hinami took the mask out of her drawer, she'd told me to come with her for the second time that day, grabbed my arm, and dragged me to a pasta restaurant near her house.

"We *are* going to use it to hide your face, but the important part is what you do after that."

What I do after that? ...But that's not what I wanted to know.

"No, wait a second, I'm asking you why we came to this restaurant all of a sudden?"

"Oh look, here it comes." She ignored my confused question as the waiter brought us our food.

"Here you go. One Japanese-style pasta with mushrooms, and one three-cheese carbonara."

He put down the carbonara in front of Hinami and the mushroom pasta in front of me.

"Come on, answer my question."

"This place is really good."

She smiled in utter bliss. Did she have to smile like that? It was insanely cute.

"...That's not what I'm talking about."

"Just listen for a minute," she said with a sigh, pointing at her mouth. She did the same trick as before, switching between her beautiful and ordinary selves.

"Oooh." *Blink blink.* "No, really, what is going on?!"

"You really are stubborn. I was just hungry, okay?"

She took a bite of her carbonara. I watched her wind the pasta around her fork, watched the arc travel to her mouth, and then watched her mouth open slightly to accept the coil of noodles before she pulled the empty fork out again. Every move was graceful and beautiful and charmingly sexy. I couldn't help following her tongue with my eyes as it swept off the sauce clinging to the corners of her mouth.

"...So good!" she murmured softly with an innocent smile.

She was seriously, insanely cute.

"In other words...it's all in the expression."

Expression? "You mean your smile just now?"

"Huh? My smile just now?"

"Oh, um, never mind."

She was so cute I accidentally put my foot in my mouth. Thankfully, Hinami kept talking like she hadn't really noticed.

"Are you listening? This is my pretty-girl mouth."

I looked more closely. The corners of her mouth were slightly lifted, and her cheeks seemed firmer as a result. She was inarguably attractive. Approachable, too. But as I stared at her, I noticed something else. *Can't put my finger on it. Must be her genuine cuteness.* When I paid attention to that, I couldn't look her in the eye, though.

"And this is my not-pretty mouth."

The spirit disappeared from her entire face. Looking closely, I noticed her mouth droop and her forehead sag. Wrinkles even formed around her nose. She wasn't ugly, but she was right on the line between beautiful and not.

"Ooo."

Blink, blink.

"Why are you oooing? You look dumb. Now's not the time to act impressed."

"...Oh right." I felt a little intimidated. *Yeah, maybe not so cute.*

"Do you get it?"

She smiled.

"This is how I look on a daily basis."

She relaxed her mouth.

"And this is how you look."

"I-I'm really that bad?"

She'd caught me off guard. I didn't think I went around smiling all the time, but wasn't it a bit much to compare me to the bad example?

"Yes, you are."

As if she'd been expecting my reaction, she thrust a mirror in my face. I saw my droopy cheeks in the reflection.

"...Oh."

"Do you see now?" I did, unfortunately. "...Apparently so."

"I still don't think that would make much of a difference. The corners of my mouth aren't the only thing that's ugly."

"You sure like to talk back."

"What do you expect? I've been thinking this stuff for sixteen years."

"For now, let's table the question of whether you're ugly."

That was nice of her. Sometimes, she could be surprisingly kind.

"I think you don't understand the importance of the mouth," she continued.

"It's important?"

"Yes."

She'd started taking bites of her pasta between sentences, and I followed her lead. *Oh wow, this is good. Crazy good. What is this place? It's incredible.*

The aroma of the soy sauce melding with perfectly browned butter reached my nose and scored a direct hit. I took a bite, appreciating the combination of the fat oozing from the bacon and the savory flavor of the mushrooms on my tongue. The rich flavors were spreading through me while my mouth was enjoying the springy texture of the noodles.

"...This...is so good...!"

I had no idea pasta this good even existed... Thank you, Hinami...

I looked at her, trying to silently convey how impressed and apprecia-tive I was. Her eyes were clouded with intense greed.

"So yours is good, too, huh?" she said calmly, her eyes flickering from my face to my pasta and back.

Um, so... Even someone with a communication block could figure out what to do in this situation.

"...Want a bite?"

She opened her eyes wide and made a face a little too cute to look at straight on.

"Thank you! Sure!" she said, sticking her fork into my pasta and spin-ning it around. She brought it to her mouth and gobbled it down. Her enraptured expression was practically carnal bliss.

Just before I could fall completely under her spell, I belatedly realized what had happened.

"Aaah!!"

"What?" Hinami asked with confusion.

Wait. Wasn't that—? Didn't our mouths just indirectly—you know? Isn't that what just happened...?!

"No, I mean, you... That was...an indirect...kiss..."

I took a lot of effort to spit the words out, but Hinami raised her eye-brows disdainfully.

"Come on. Maybe if we were sharing a bottle of water or something, but no one worries about little things like that after junior high."

"Really? Oh, um, people don't usually worry about it...?"

"Yeah. Anyway, as I was saying," she continued, ignoring my shock and assuming a businesslike attitude.

"Imagine two men wearing sunglasses are having a conversation. Their eyes and eyebrows are hidden. You can't hear what they're saying, but you can see them."

"What are you talking about now?"

I was still upset about the indirect kiss thing, but damn, this pasta was good.

"One is a normie and the other isn't. Do you think you could tell which was which just from their appearance?"

Are we still talking about mouths? Let's see, two men wearing sunglasses...

"Uh...well, I guess if I saw them, I could figure it out—God, this is good—from their hair or the way they acted or their clothes," I said between bites of my heavenly plate of pasta.

"What if they both had buzz cuts and suits?"

Buzz cuts and suits... I tried to picture it. Two guys with buzz cuts wearing sunglasses...in suits...*munch, munch*...talking to each other.

"I think I'd still be able to tell."

Hinami nodded. "Right. Same hair, eyes and eyebrows hidden. You can still basically tell which is which. Isn't that strange?"

"I guess so. This is delicious, by the way. That *is* kind of strange."

"Why do you think you can tell them apart? ...Here's the answer."

She pointed to her mouth. *No way.*

"...Pasta?"

"Idiot."

Yeah, that was dumb. Sorry.

"...Facial expression?"

"That's it."

"Uh-huh..."

"Like I showed you before, your expression, especially your mouth, makes a huge difference in people's impression of you. They pick up on it subconsciously and use it to make judgments about your personality."

Yeah, I guess so.

"Sounds reasonable enough," I said, before suddenly realizing something. "But wait a second. Is that the reason you're always smiling?" I couldn't help shoving another bite of pasta into my mouth.

"Kind of. You're half-right, half-wrong."

"Half?"

"At first, I made a conscious effort to smile, but as my muscles developed, it started happening naturally. Yeah, this *is* good... It took a couple of months to get to that point, though."

"A couple months..."

So much effort lay behind that friendly appearance. "Anyway, you're saying your facial muscles and mouth are important, right? ...But what's the mask for? If I hide my mouth, won't I lose all the benefits?"

"It's like weight training."

"Huh?"

"Weight training. They're muscles, so if you want to build them, you've gotta train."

"...What are you talking about?" I asked, puzzled.

Hinami pushed a pack of thirty masks against my chest. "For the next month, whenever you're not eating or sleeping—when you're out and about, when you're in class, when you're talking to someone—I want you to have a huge smile on your face under the mask the whole time."

"...What?! Seriously? The whole time?" I asked, bewildered, as I took the masks from her.

"Obviously. We don't have forever. I want you to be done in a month."

Hinami sat back down. Somehow, her plate was already empty.

"Hey, you said it took you a couple of months. Why can't I go at the same pace?"

"Don't be silly. You'd never make your goal."

"My goal?" That was the first time I'd heard her say that word. "To become a normie?"

"Don't you know how it works? When you're going to start working toward something, it's important to have a big, long-term goal, but you need mid-term and short-term goals, too."

"...Oh." Yeah, when I was practicing *Atafami*, I did set those kinds of goals.

"You of all people should know that."

"...Yeah, I guess I do."

"That's what I thought. You're picking this up quick."

When I want to reach a big goal, I progress a lot more smoothly if I have a bunch of smaller goals to achieve. More like if I don't, then I don't know how to move forward, and then my motivation disappears. At least, that's been the case when I was mastering various games.

And since life is a game, too, I should take the same approach.

"You're going to move forward by clearing a series of small, medium, and big goals."

"So I should think of my big goal as…becoming a normie?"

"Right. Of course, there are different levels of normie, your final goal should be to reach my level."

"Isn't that…a little too hard?"

"I admit, it's a long way to go—the biggest loner in school to the most successful in the real world. But if you do exactly what I tell you, it's not impossible."

…*Seriously?*

"Well, all right… And what about my small and medium goals?"

"Right. First I'll tell you your small goals."

Gulp.

"Get your family or close friends to ask if you have a girlfriend."

…*Huh?*

"What do you mean?"

"What I said."

"Huh?"

Hinami looked at me, clearly annoyed by my confusion. "Geez… You're so quick to catch on with *Atafami* and so slow when it comes to real life."

She turned her palms up and gave an exaggerated sigh.

"That's none of your business," I said.

"Can we go on? I'm talking about surface changes so big people around you notice and ask you about them."

Hmm…surface changes big enough for people to notice and ask?

"…And they have to ask if I have a girlfriend?"

"Oh geez. It doesn't matter *what*, exactly; it could be 'I almost didn't recognize you for a second' or 'Damn, you glowed up!' The point is, you've cleared the level once people start saying they notice a big change in you."

"I—I see."

"The part about *other* people saying something is important. It's not enough just for you to think you've changed a lot."

"Um-hmm."

"It means you have to get to a point where people are objectively looking at you and seeing a clear improvement in your appearance. In the aura you give off."

"U-understood."

Hinami was annoyed; I could tell from the wrinkle between her brows. "Do I have to explain every little detail?"

"S-sorry...but how do I know..."

"Know what?"

"Even if the people around me say something, how do I know I've really passed?"

"...Can you not even make that decision yourself?"

"S-sorry."

"...Fine. If someone says something, repeat it to me word for word, and I'll decide if it counts."

"O-okay."

A feeling of reluctance and shame washed over me.

"Once you've cleared that goal, I'll give you the next small goal. It'll depend on how you're doing then. And about the mid-range goal...well, that's a simple one."

She smiled.

"Have a girlfriend by the time you start your third year of high school."

My jaw dropped. A girlfriend? Me? The guy who's been a lone wolf from day one? She must have assumed I didn't already have one because, well, I'm me. She was right, of course.

"No. Nope. No way."

"What?"

"That's way too hard."

"What's too hard about it?" She genuinely didn't seem to understand.

"You probably don't get it because having a boyfriend is easy for you, but for those of us who aren't so popular, that's a crazy thing to expect. Plus, it's June already, right? Which means I have less than a year! It's totally impossible!"

Without even meaning to, I'd stood up to deliver a passionate lecture on my own unpopularity. The waiter, bringing our tea, smirked as he set the saucers on the table. Hinami sighed from her seat. God, how embarrassing.

"Huh? ...Okay, let me ask you a question."

Her eyes were very, *very* cold.

"Uh, okay."

"What percentage of guys in their second year of high school have a girlfriend, do you think?"

"Um... What, maybe twenty or thirty percent?"

"...Okay, let's go on the low end and say ten percent."

"Okay..." *What is she getting at?*

"Let's compare this to a video game to help you understand. We'll say *Atafami*. You're the best in Japan, right?"

"Um, I guess."

"Okay, then let's imagine there's a total beginner who wants to master *Atafami*. That's where you come in." She pointed at me sternly.

"Me?"

"Yeah. You have one year to give this person all the advice they need, like how to control the characters and how to practice. They promise to do exactly as you say."

"...Okay..."

"How hard do you think it would be to make sure that person is among the top ten percent of all players in Japan in one year?"

The top 10 percent. That means a one-in-ten level, probably the best in their class. Which means, well...

"...Super...easy."

"Hexactly."

"Huh?"

"It's easy, even when we set the number down at ten percent. In other words, if you do what I say, you'll have no problem finding a girlfriend by the time you advance to the next level," she explained, speaking quickly.

"Wait, what did you say before that?"

"...You're imagining things."

Huh? Is she messing with me? Her face was red. *Is she making fun of me and trying not to laugh?* I seemed to remember hearing those words before...

"Let's focus on what's important. Do you understand what I'm saying? It's not a very difficult goal."

Okay, maybe in terms of raw logic, but...

"But *Atafami* and life are different."

That earned me another sigh. "Would you stop assuming things? You may be a pro at *Atafami*, but you're an amateur at life. If you're actually planning give it a try, just follow my advice."

"...Sorry. Um, you're right."

I deferred to her and apologized. After all, I was the one who'd decided to play. She was right—I didn't know the rules of life or how to skillfully handle the characters. A top expert was telling me what to do, so for now I figured I'd better just obey her every instruction. That's what a gamer should do. I could decide later whether life was the god-tier game she said it was.

"Do you know where Sewing Classroom Number Two is?"

"Huh?"

"Sewing Classroom Number Two, in the old school building. Know where it is?"

Oh, she was talking about our school... It sounded familiar. I thought I remembered; I could probably find it if I went to the old building.

"Yeah, basically."

"Good. From now on, go to that room half an hour before school starts every day, and then again after school."

"Why?"

"So I can tell you what to do that day, and later you can report back and reflect on how you did. Obviously. What's training without trial and error? If we're doing this, we're gonna do it right."

If we're doing this, we're gonna do it right. Well…I could agree with her there.

"…Roger that."

"Of course, some days one of us will have plans, so we'll cross those bridges when we come to them. You have my e-mail address, right?"

"Yeah. But I hardly ever have plans. Ha-ha."

"…Okay, are you gonna take this seriously or not? A few months from now, you *will* have plans after school. Are you ready for that?"

She glared at me. *Wait, really?*

"Seriously?"

"Obviously."

She sounded super-sure of herself. If she was right, that would be pretty cool.

"I understand. I'm ready." I bowed my head slightly.

"Oh, and…"

Suddenly, she sounded flustered, and all but a trace of her coolness was gone. She sipped her tea and looked to the side.

"Huh? What?"

She jumped a little, like she was startled. What was her deal?

"Well, um, this was officially an offline meeting between NO NAME and nanashi, right?"

Why are you so shy all of a sudden? "Y-yeah. What's wrong?"

"Wh-what do you mean, what's wrong? …You know, it's an offline meeting…"

"What?"

"Oh, come on!" she said, sounding a lot more worked up than usual. She glanced down for a second, took a breath, then made eye contact so deliberate it felt almost unnatural.

"I mean, wouldn't we normally exchange *Atafami* friend codes?"

She'd been looking me in the eye throughout our whole conversation, but now it felt like, I don't know, some kind of bluff. Like she was forcing herself to keep looking at me because to do otherwise would be to admit defeat.

Despite her sharp glare and tightly pursed lips, her cheeks were gradually getting redder. Even someone with terrible communication skills like me could tell it wasn't from heat or anger. Still, that doesn't mean I knew how to respond. *She did say earlier that she gets worked up when it comes to Atafami, but I didn't know it was this bad.*

"That's all… You look like you want to say something."

I had no intention of kicking the hornet's nest, so I just told her, "Whatever, that's fine," and exchanged friend codes with her. Now we'd be able to play friendlies any time.

I would never forget the way she was blushing, but I knew I shouldn't think about it too much.

Oh, and by the way, even the tea at that pasta place was to die for.

2

It feels awesome to gain a bunch of levels after a battle

It was forty minutes before school started. I'd given myself time to spare, since I didn't know exactly where Sewing Room #2 was, but I found it more easily than I expected and got there ten minutes early.

The room had an old-fashioned feel to it, and the blackboard's claim that it was October 26 on an early summer day made it feel like some kind of abandoned ruins, but in a good way. The dust swirling busily through the rays of sunlight made the atmosphere almost magical. The sewing machines lined up at even intervals near the windows seemed to be last decade's model, which gave the room a modern feel, contrary to what you'd expect. The ceramic surface must have been white once, but now they were yellowed from the sun, and something about the color evoked a brief feeling of nostalgia.

As I was soaking up the quiet morning, Hinami came in.

"Good morning, Tomozaki-kun. Today's the big day one, huh?"

"Uh, yeah."

"The atmosphere in here's kinda neat, don't you think?" She looked around.

"Uh, um, yeah. It's not bad. Kinda feels like ruins."

"Wow, you get it. You've got good taste. I wanted to choose somewhere good since we'll be coming here a lot," she explained, sitting down. "The chairs are uncomfortable, though."

She smiled. I sat down opposite her on one of the rickety stools. She was right—it wasn't very comfortable.

"I don't mind that. I actually like retro games and board games."

"Really? I'd love to play you some time."

"With pleasure. If you think *Atafami*'s all I'm good at, you're in for a nasty surprise."

"Ha-ha, I don't think that… But *you* might be the one in for a surprise."

For an instant, we had a clash of pride as nanashi and NO NAME.

"Anyway…what's on the agenda for today?"

"…Right. Let's get down to business. For now, in order to reach your first small goal, just keep up the mask strength training… And for your medium goal, I'd like to start testing the waters."

"And that medium goal is…finding a girlfriend…"

Honestly speaking, it still didn't feel real.

"How do you manage to be so obnoxious even with a mask on? Must be your own special gift."

"That's none of your business."

"Anyway, it's clear what today's assignment should be."

"Uh-oh…" *Gulp.*

"…Today, your job is to talk to at least three girls at school."

Um… "Well, that sounds easy… But I'm starting field practice already?"

So far, the only thing I'd done was train my facial muscles, and I'd barely started that.

"Did you have a question?"

"No, I mean, isn't it a little soon? Nothing about me has changed, yet, so…"

I could understand talking to girls once I'd practiced talking in general or finished my face training, but if I did it now, wouldn't they just call me a creep?

"I understand your concern. But this is necessary right now, so just do it."

"Well…okay." I'd already decided that if I was going to do this, I'd obey her completely.

"There are a couple of important points you need to watch out for, though."

"Important points?"

"Yep. First is what you talk about, and I have some guidelines for that."

"Like what?"

"It's gotta be something like, 'I've got a cold and I ran out of tissues; could I have one of yours if you have any?' Doesn't matter if it's tissues or something else, but the cold should be your icebreaker."

"So anything goes as long as I start with the cold?"

"Right. When you talk to someone you've never talked to before, you need an immediately visible reason, or else they'll be wary of you. Especially if you're at the bottom of the class hierarchy. They'll wonder why you're suddenly talking to them. It's not a problem if you can strike up a natural-sounding conversation, but knowing you, you'd probably say something weird. Since they'll see your mask right away, it's perfectly normal to say you have a cold."

She did insult me in the middle of her little explanation, but it was still convincing.

"Worst case, if you screw it up by acting creepy and the girl backs off, you can fix it later. She'll probably blame it on the cold and change her opinion of you, right?"

"R-right…"

She'd even considered the possibility of a pathetic failure. *Thank you very much. I'll probably need that.*

"There's one more thing to be careful about. Make sure you talk to them when I'm nearby."

"Why do you have to be nearby? Is that because you want to make sure I actually talk to three girls?"

"Uh…well, pretty much." She was surprisingly strict.

"Okay."

"Good answer."

"Oh, do you think I'll even have three chances to naturally talk to a girl while you're nearby?"

"Definitely. You can talk to Yuzu before homeroom because she sits next to you. Yuzu Izumi. Then there's Mimimi in home ec, when we change classrooms—Minami Nanami, I mean. You won't have to go out of your way to talk to ther."

"...You really remember who I sit next to."

"Oh, I always memorize where everyone sits when we get new seating arrangements."

Weird. But impressive. She's right that I should have time to talk to those two if I make an effort... *But...*

"...What about number three?"

"Can't you take a little initiative during lunch or something?"

"Oh right."

This was gonna be hard.

Our strategy meeting ended on that note, and I returned to our classroom a couple of minutes after Hinami. That was when I realized it was now or never for me to carry out my assignment of talking to Yuzu Izumi. *I am not emotionally prepared for this. Whoo boy.*

I mean, think about it. Yuzu Izumi, of all people? She was one of the "cool kids." She wasn't the boss or anything, but she was cheerful and loud and laughed a lot—the bright and happy type. Some days she wore a necktie, which was also proof of her coolness.

Here at Sekitomo High School, girls can wear either a ribbon or a necktie, but there seems to be an unspoken understanding passed down from year to year that unpopular girls are not allowed to wear the neckties. Yuzu Izumi apparently doesn't care which she wears and switches back and forth whenever she feels like it, which suggests she's fairly comfortable in her position.

By the way, our school's very modern attitude toward the dress code is popular with the students, but some people think it's stupid to be out here flexing in the middle of our rice fields. Such is the fate of Saitama.

Well, anyway. Yuzu Izumi wears her skirt short, and whether she's going for the ribbon or the tie that day, she ties it loose and pairs it with a bright cardigan. She's like a model cool girl. The kind of girl rumored to flirt with all the boys. She's got big boobs, too. She's neat and tidy and cute, which makes her less intimidating, but still, I was supposed to say something to Yuzu Izumi out of the blue? It would be impossible without a cold for an excuse, definitely.

When I got to my seat, Yuzu Izumi was digging through her bag like she was looking for something. Once she found it, she would probably get up and go over by the window to join the group of cool kids hanging out there. That meant now was my only chance. Hinami was in sight, too... *Here I go. Hope this goes okay!*

"Um, e-excuse me, Izumi-san, uh..."

"Huh? Oh, Tomozaki-kun? You need something?"

To no one's surprise, she looked a little confused by the fact that I'd spoken to her. Still, I could sense how bright and cheery she was just from the perky way she turned toward me. The little gap between her buttons gave me a glimpse of her boobs. The buttons were under stress from her large chest, and taut horizontal wrinkles had formed between them and her armpits. In other words, her top was so tight I couldn't help picturing the curvature of her boobs. They were huge. Why did normie girls always wear such tight shirts? Did they buy them a size too small on purpose? I wish they wouldn't, because I can't stop looking.

"Uh, um, do you have a tissue? I have a cold, but I forgot mine..."

I was trying to act sick, struggling desperately to avoid looking at her chest, and training my grin under the mask, so I have no idea what my voice sounded like.

"Oh, um, wait a second... Oh sorry, I don't have any!"

She brought her palms together in an apologetic pose. The way she pressed her arms in made her big chest even more pronounced. *Not looking, not looking.* But she'd answered casually, like a regular "Oops!" to someone in her cool group. She'd treated me more like an ordinary human being than I'd expected. That was a relief.

"Oh, okay. Sorry, it's okay."

Even as the words left my mouth, I was thinking, *What am I saying? "Sorry, it's okay"?*

A second later, Yuzu Izumi swiveled around to the seat behind her and did something surprising. "Hey, got a tissue?"

Whoa, that was unexpected. Very unexpected. Her reflexes when it came to interpersonal relationships were incredible. I mean, look how she instinctively asked another person for a tissue. Was I ready for this?

"Yes, I do… Please, help yourself…," the girl replied gently, then immediately offered a packet of tissues. It was all happening so fast. Did she keep a pack of tissues constantly at the ready on her desk or something?

Um, that's Fuka Kikuchi-san, right?

I could give a quick, generic description like "artsy type with fair skin and short black hair," but that wouldn't do justice to her unique, sensitive aura and fairylike presence. One glance was enough to know she was beautiful. She had a habit of looking down, which highlighted her long eyelashes. For some reason, she used formal, polite language even with her classmates.

"Thanks! Here you go."

Yuzu Izumi cheerfully took the tissues from Kikuchi-san and held them out to me.

"Th-thanks."

I threw a quick glance at each of them in turn to express my gratitude. That was all the sincerity I was capable of.

Yuzu Izumi must have found what she'd been looking for while she was searching for the tissues. She picked up a small hand mirror, stood up, threw me a quick "Bye," and walked over to her friends.

That left me suddenly face-to-face with Kikuchi-san. I still hadn't blown my nose. Since she'd handed me the whole packet, I wouldn't be free until I blew my nose and gave the rest back.

Kikuchi-san was looking absently in my direction, apparently because she didn't have anything else to look at. This was oddly awkward. I wanted to just pretend to blow my nose and return the tissues as quickly as possible, but her look was so odd—absent-minded, maybe, but also strong. Her black eyes glittered strangely, like treasures in a dense jungle.

I'd sat down sideways in my chair, which meant that when I blew my nose Kikuchi-san's glittering eyes would take in the whole thing. But turning to face forward would be awkward, too, since it could seem overly deliberate. I decided to stay where I was, pull the mask away, and blow my nose. Kikuchi-san probably felt like looking away would imply something, so she absently watched me blowing my nose with her mysterious eyes. *What is going on?* A minor drama born of our unwillingness to move.

After the deed was done, I looked at Kikuchi-san. She shifted her gaze away slightly.

"…Um, thanks."

"…You're welcome."

If you'd only seen this part of the interaction, you'd think we were a happy, innocent pair of kids. After me blowing my nose, not so much. I solemnly handed back the packet of tissues, then went to throw away the one I'd used and returned to my seat. Mission accomplished. I was wondering if I would be able to count this as talking to two girls when…

"Tomozaki-kun."

"Ah!"

I was startled by Kikuchi-san's clear voice, which felt like a breeze blowing down my ear and hitting my brain.

"Wh-what?"

"Um…"

Had I done something wrong? She seemed extremely dubious.

"Um…I wanted to ask you…"

"Yeah…?"

"Um…why…"

Why what…?

"Why…were you smiling?"

Ha-ha-ha… Shit.

In the end, I managed to save myself with some incoherent answer about my teeth hurting, which made me pull my lips back into something that looked like a smile, but Kikuchi-san's frown when she had asked the question and the confusion in her eyes made me think I probably didn't convince her of anything.

When I glanced at Hinami to see what she thought of this little exchange, she gave a dramatic sigh. *Yup, I screwed that one up. Kikuchi-san thinks I'm a creep.* Still, details aside, I'd fulfilled the basic requirements of the assignment. All I could do was view this as a big step forward and consider how to do better next time.

Next up was fourth-period home ec. Once again, I was a nervous wreck. Now I had to talk to Minami Nanami, who goes by Mimimi or Nanana. She got both nicknames because her whole name only uses two different syllables. Apparently, she mostly goes by Mimimi these days. She's a classic Japanese beauty—pale skin, long black hair, and even, defined features—but for someone with such a traditional aesthetic, she has a bright, cheerful personality. She's on the track team with Hinami.

Whenever we have to switch classrooms and I get there too early, the other loners are usually sitting at their desks thumbing through their textbooks or notes, trying to play at being cool and disinterested in the others. I don't like to get involved in that, so I always kill time by going to the library first.

Not many people go to a library on a ten-minute break, so it's usually either just me or me and one other person. By the way, I only pretend to read the books—I'm really working on tactics for *Atafami*. But today, I didn't have time to go to the library. I had to get to class as early as possible to talk to Minami Nanami, or maybe, if I had the chance, to another girl.

The moment third period ended, I grabbed my home-ec textbook and workbook, my pencils, and some loose-leaf paper and left the classroom.

As expected, the air of the home-ec room hung thick with apathy—with an extra twist. Two loners were sitting apart from each other, as well as a relevant party—I mean the person who sits next to me—I mean— Okay, I'll just say it: my target, Minami Nanami. *Oh, come on!* She had her workbook open and mechanical pencil at work. This was definitely an opportunity, but if I talked to her now, when the classroom was otherwise silent, our voices would be the only sounds in the room. I didn't mind if the two loners overheard us, but I didn't like the idea of my own voice filling the room. I know that's irrational, but it's true.

This was tough. What to do? I would rather have waited... *Oh wait,*

Hinami isn't here yet. Yeah, I'm supposed to do it when she was watching, so I can't do it yet. Oh well, I'll just have to wait a little longer. Until some more people come in.

By the time I sat down next to Minami Nanami, I'd prepared a hundred excuses and was in a safe mental state.

"Hey, what's up Tomozaki-kun? You're early today, aren't you!"

Oh, come on*!*

A second ago she'd been silently focused on her workbook, but the instant I sat down, she started talking to me like it was the most natural thing in the world. The whole flow was so smooth that it took a second for it to register that she had talked to me at all. But no, she had definitely said my name.

I couldn't ignore her, but if I told her the real reason I'd come so early—specifically to talk to her—I'd look like such a freak she'd probably kill me. Unfortunately, I'm the opposite of a witty conversationalist.

So…

"…No…"

"Huh?"

"…No, um, it wasn't on purpose."

"Oh really? Well, yeah, that's usually how it goes, isn't it?"

…that's how our conversation went.

Wow, all I said was "it wasn't on purpose," which was completely pointless, and she still answered "Well, yeah." …I've gotta say, young women these days really have an amazing ability to empathize. Wonder if I'll ever get to that point.

But what to do now? A conversation had begun, which meant that if we fell back into silence, the mood would give its divine verdict: that we were not each doing our own work, but that we had started a conversation and couldn't continue it. It goes without saying that I didn't have any safe topics on hand, such as the latest episode of a show or gossip about so-and-so in our class. Worst case, I could ask her for a tissue as if the need had just occurred to me, but that would be a little weird.

With awkwardness pressing in on me, my only choice was to muddle through.

"Wow, that was amazing," I timidly offered, trying to make my voice as nonchalant as possible.

"Huh? What was?"

Nanami-san blankly stared with her round eyes. Her voice was clear but very loud, which meant it reached the whole classroom.

"Um, I mean, all I said was 'it wasn't on purpose,' which didn't really mean anything."

"Huh?" She was confused. Of course she was.

"But you still managed to agree with me…and it made me think about how this generation has amazing powers of empathy…"

Nanami-san was silent, as if her brain hadn't yet fully processed what I was saying. No surprises there. I'd just said exactly what was on my mind a second ago. This conversation was shit.

"…"

"…"

Awkward. Well, this is hopeless. Now everything was weird, and it was completely my fault. There was no saving this. *How are you supposed to make conversation? She told me to talk to girls, so I did, and look where that got me.*

"Uh, sorr—"

"Ah-ha-ha-ha-ha-ha!"

"Huh?"

She was really losing it. The other two kids in the classroom kept glancing toward us.

"Uh, wh-wha—"

"What are you talking about, Tomozaki-kun! You sound like an old man! Ha-ha-ha-ha!"

Wh-what's going on? "Um, I was just saying this generation…"

"But *you're* this generation, too! Ah-ha-ha-ha!"

"No, I was just…"

"…What? Just what?" she asked eagerly, still giggling. *I'm trying to say something serious!*

"Like, high school girls these days use words like 'yikes' to mean all different things, right…? So I was thinking empathy is becoming more common for girls in this…"

"Ah-ha-ha-ha-ha! Stop! Stop talking like a talk show host! Ha-ha-ha!"

The more seriously I tried to explain, the more hilarious it was. What was going on? While she was busy laughing at me, other students had started trickling into the classroom and looking at us with curiousity. *Tomozaki and Mimimi?!!*

"No, it's just, like, I heard about it somewhere, but it didn't sound like a real thing, and when I saw it for myself, it sort of gave the theory more punch..."

"Ah-ha-ha-ha! You're killing me!"

"I just thought it was a valuable example..."

"That's what I'm talking about—you sound like an old man! You literally live in the middle of examples! Ah-ha-ha-ha!"

"Minmi, what's going on?"

Hanabi Natsubayashi, who was in our half of the class for home ec, had sat down across from Nanami-san. She's petite and delicate, with bobbed hair, a childlike face, and very compact little movements, like a squirrel.

"Hi, Tama! Still tiny, I see!" Nanami-san said, ruffling Natsubayashi-san's hair. I'm not sure how it started, but everyone calls her "Tama," like the popular name for cats. Tama calls Nanami-san Minmi. I don't know where that came from, either.

"Cut it out! Just answer my question!"

Natsubayashi-san pushed Nanami-san's arm away with one hand and scolded her sharply from her height of less than five feet. Still, there wasn't much real bite to her harsh-sounding reply.

"You're scary, Tama!"

"Don't change the subject! Explain!"

"Sorry, sorry. Tomozaki-kun's talking like an old man. He said—what did you say? I forgot!"

"Huh?!"

"Hee-hee-hee. Guess you shoulda got here earlier!"

"That's not true! You! Uh, Tomozaki, right? Tell me what happened!"

Next, she turned her razor-sharp tongue on me, but what cut deep was the way she kind of forgot my name.

"Who, me?"

"Is there another Tomozaki around?"

"No…"

"Then stop dawdling!"

"Good luck, Tomozaki!" Nanami-san joked with both fists pressed to her cheeks.

"What do you mean, good luck…? Uh… Um…"

I bumbled through an explanation. In the meantime, Hinami had come into the home-ec room with a few friends, smiling. When she saw what was going on she froze for a couple of seconds, then quickly recovered.

"…and that's what happened."

"Ah-ha-ha-ha-ha!"

"That's not funny at all," Natsubayashi-san said.

"What? It's hilarious!"

"No it's not! You're just crazy!"

"Ooh, you're so mean! Ah-ha-ha!"

"Stop laughing!"

Natsubayashi-san really seemed to enjoy cutting Nanami-san down. Not a shred of empathy. I guess not everyone in our generation is the same. Anyway, Nanami-san had laughed at me when I was trying to be serious, so I was on Natsubayashi-san's side.

"Um, I don't think it's funny, either…"

"What?!"

"Right? Like I said, Minmi, you're crazy!"

"Aw, I wouldn't say that! You just don't understand 'cause you're a child!" Nanami-san said.

"Shut up! You're so annoying!"

"Ha-ha-ha, look at you! Come on, Tomozaki, wouldn't you say Tama's a child?"

Huh? She's asking me?! Is she a child? I don't think so, but I have no idea what to say. What do I do? I'm not smooth enough for this. My only choice was to say what I was thinking again.

"Um…uh…I don't know if she's a child."

"Of course you do!"

"Um, yes…but, like, what I felt before was… You had amazing powers of empathy, but just now, Natsubayashi-san shot you down, right? So everyone is different, and you can't make snap judgments about all young women…"

"Ah-ha-ha-ha-ha-ha! Listen to him!"

"…"

Nanami-san exploded with laughter, while Natsubayashi-san glowered up at me, disgruntled.

"So the conclusion I can draw is that you shouldn't generalize based on a single example… That's about it…"

"Stop already! Ah-ha-ha!"

As usual, Nanami-san was cracking up. Natsubayashi-san ignored her deafening laughter and addressed me.

"…That…"

"Huh?"

"…That *was* kinda funny!"

What was?

"Mimimi and Hanabi and…Tomozaki? What're you guys all worked up about?"

In the middle of our muddled conversation, I heard a familiar voice. I was so flustered I'd forgotten the time, and I hadn't noticed someone coming up to us, either. Actually, though, I'd predicted this, and it was exactly what I was afraid of. I should have wrapped up this conversation sooner.

Tomozaki, Natsubayashi, Nanami. We sit in order of our student numbers in home ec. And between Tomozaki and Natsubayashi was—

—Nakamura.

"What's up with you two? Having fun with Tomozaki, huh?"

He walked up to us, frowning moodily and flanked by two other guys from his group, Mizusawa and…Takeishi, I think? They were both solid members of the so-called Nakamura Faction, with Nakamura at the center and the other two backing him up. Mizusawa in particular wasn't just a follower but more like a key advisor. Even I could tell he was a sly operator.

"Hey Nakamu, listen to him! Tomozaki is really hilarious…"

"Oh really? Tomozaki is?" Nakamura glanced at me. His mouth was grinning. His eyes were not. "Whaddaya mean?"

His eyes glittered like those of a snake ready to sink its fangs into my heart. What was he planning to do to me?

A week had already passed since our *Atafami* showdown. The tension back when everyone had basically guessed what happened had dissipated, but right now, he had his followers with him, which meant he'd probably want to look even tougher than usual.

"He sounds just like an old guy on a talk show!"

"What? An old guy on a talk show?" he asked grumpily.

"Yeah!"

"I don't get it," Nakamura said.

Mizusawa, who was standing next to him, turned his gaze to me without moving his head. "Tell us about it, Tomozaki!" he said.

Maybe he had guessed Nakamura's intentions; he directed the question straight at me. I didn't like the way he called me by my name. Did he think I'd start stuttering if I had to say more than a few words? Was he playing with me? *Don't underestimate me, man. I may not be smooth, but I can explain myself just fine. Plus, I'm a hell of a lot better than you guys at Atafami.*

And explain myself I did.

"…So that's what happened."

"Ah-ha-ha. See what I mean?"

Not surprisingly, Nanami-san didn't laugh as hard this time, since this was the second time she'd heard it. As for Natsubayashi-san, she'd been silent ever since Nakamura and his crew showed up. Was she intimidated because three popular guys were there?

"...And?" Nakamura said when I finished talking.

"Huh?"

"That's it?"

"Yeah..."

"That's not funny."

He turned to his two followers.

"Right?"

"Yup, not funny at all...," Takei agreed gravely.

Mizusawa looked at him and started cackling loudly. "Ah-hah-hah!"

"You guys have a weird sense of humor," Nanami-san commented,

"Uh, that would be you!" Nakamura shot back.

"What?! Nanamu, you're harsh!"

Everyone except me and Natsubayashi-san was cracking up. Things were getting very uncomfortable. I started thinking the only reason this was still bearable at all was thanks to Nanami-san's comical expression and tone.

"Okay then...should we vote on it?" Mizusawa proposed.

"Brilliant," Nakamura said, like a general bowing to his tactician.

"...Uh-oh, this feels like a setup...," Nanami-san said, laughing.

"Okay! Who thinks Mimimi's a weirdo?"

Takei enthusiastically took a vote, acting like this was finally his big moment. Nakamura, Takei, and Mizusawa raised their hands.

"Ah-ha-ha-ha! Hey!" Nanami-san joked. I got the sense she was spinning her wheels, but if she hadn't been, I think I might have suffocated.

"Damn, we don't have a majority," Mizusawa joked back.

"Wait, those guys didn't vote, so we don't know yet!"

...A bizarre game had begun. What was I supposed to do? First of all, I didn't like the idea of joining in this weird voting game. They'd probably say it was more playing around than bullying, but I'm bad at judging these things. Plus, Natsubayashi-san was getting grumpy. Intimidation didn't explain it. What relationships were at play here?

"Oh, come on, Nakamu! You sure look like you know!"

"Okay, who thinks Shuji's a weirdo?"

Nanami-san thrust her hand into the air comically. Natsubayashi-san kept staring at the ground, ignoring what was happening. Something out of the ordinary was definitely going on. I examined everyone's expressions and tried to figure out what it was. *What is this? What am I supposed to do?*

I thought about it in my own totally-inexperienced-with-human-relationships way.

...If I didn't raise my hand now, they'd definitely ask me why I hadn't voted for either one. And given what I'd observed so far, if they asked Natsubayashi-san the same thing, there was a high likelihood she'd ignore them. Which meant that my decision to raise my hand or not at this point would determine whether Natsubayashi-san was the one they started needling for not voting.

In other words, if I raised my hand, Natsubayashi-san would be left all alone. If I didn't, there would be two of us to tease. And I'd be the main target of their attack. Which meant it would be wiser for me not to raise my hand. Yeah, definitely. *I'm keeping my hand down.*

But what is this about, anyway? How did Natsubayashi-san end up in this position? Why is Natsumi still laughing? Does she not realize what was happening? Or is it not really a big deal, and I'm just overreacting? God, I have no clue! Group conversations are way too hard!!

"Hey! I vote for Nakamura, too!"

Just then, I heard a cheerful, friendly voice behind me.

No—an overly cheerful, overly friendly, and definitely fake voice.

"You don't even know what we're talking about, Aoi." Nakamura's tone was cheerful but also threatening.

"Aww, but I was listening to the whole thing from over there. I thought I could vote, too."

"No way. This is a Group 4 issue. Bye-bye, outsider."

Nakamura flapped his hands like he was sweeping Hinami away. Her too-perfect smile remained firmly in place.

*   *   *

"Whaaaat? But you're the one who lost to Tomozaki-kun in *Atafami*."

The air froze.

Hinami had spoken in a fairly loud voice, and the topic was a minor taboo that no one in class ever brought up. Everyone else had been casually watching us ever since Nakamura arrived, so all of them heard what she said. For a second, Nanami-san's ever-present smile seemed to twitch.

"Hey, Aoi."

"Sure is cheap to use a vote to pick on someone just 'cause you're upset he beat you! That's why Shimano dumped you! She was like, 'Younger guys are *so* immature!'" Hinami changed her voice to imitate the older girl's and mimed along.

"You…just shut up."

"Ah-ha-ha-ha! You sound just like her!"

"Pfft, ha-ha!"

"Ha-ha-ha!"

Not only Nanami-san but Takei and Mizusawa were laughing. The other kids who'd been watching were giggling, too.

It was incredible.

"So with me and Mimimi, that makes two votes. Who else?" Hinami glanced at me… *Ah, I gotcha.*

"I vote for Nakamura, too."

"Oh shit!" Nakamura said. He sounded vaguely humiliated but cheerful at the same time. This was how Hinami worked. And then next…

"Hey," I said quietly, throwing Natsubayashi-san a glance.

"…"

She silently raised her hand.

"That's four votes! Looks like Shuji's the one with the weird sense of humor!"

"Nice work, Nakamu!"

Hinami and Nanami-san were teasing him, but affectionately.

"Welp, the majority has spoken," Nakamura joked, frowning.

"Bet you want revenge! You should play Tomozaki-kun in *Atafami* again!"

The whole class burst out laughing. What was going on? The taboo had suddenly become a joke. What was this?

"All right, all right! Tomozaki, I'm waiting for you!" Nakamura declared theatrically as he looked at me. When our eyes met, I saw genuine anger. Yikes. This is why I don't like to look people in the eye.

"Uh, yeah, can't wait."

The home-ec teacher arrived right then. Perfect timing.

Could Hinami have planned that, too? …No, no way.

"Thanks, Aoi! That was awesome!"

"Ha-ha, thanks, Hanabi."

As soon as Nakamura left the room after class, Natsubayashi-san ran up to Hinami and threw her arms around her.

"I was about to ruin everything again."

"Thought so. It's so easy to tell what you're thinking," Hinami said, patting Natsubayashi-san's head as she hugged her. If I'd only seen that one image, I'd have thought it was a happy scene, but that comment about being "about to ruin everything" was interesting.

"Nice job, Tama! You did good!" Nanami-san added, running up and throwing her arms around her and Hinami from behind with the same enthusiasm as Natsubayashi-san.

So there was Hinami, with Natsubayashi-san hugging her from the front and Nanami-san hugging her from behind. A cute girl snugly caught between two beautiful ones, like some gorgeous high school girl sandwich.

"Hey! Get off us!" Natsubayashi-san scolded in her typical domineering tone, but Nanami-san totally ignored her.

"You were so good! You deserve a compliment!"

Nanami-san ruffled the smaller girl's hair with both hands. When Natsubayashi-san wordlessly pushed them away, Nanami-san just moved down and ruffled her hair. Then, to my disbelief, she nibbled on Natsubayashi-san's ear.

"Eep!"

Nanami-san looked very pleased by this reaction and traced her long, slender white fingers from the base of Natsubayashi-san's neck up to the bottom of the ear and between her lips. Then, at just the right moment when Natsubayashi-san shivered, she gave her ear a lick and made her jump again.

"Hey, Minmi...! That...ah! Tick-tickles!"

Natsubayashi-san clung to Hinami, squealing as if she couldn't stand it any longer. Nanami-san, looking entranced with her eyes half closed and her cheeks red, blew out a warm breath.

"Hey, Mimimi, now you're going too far," Hinami said with some disbelief as she gently bopped Nanami-san on the head. Nanami-san looked at Hinami with the same fascination, which then turned into a smirk. Hinami stepped back slightly, but she couldn't move far with Natsubayashi-san still clinging to her. Perhaps guessing what was about to happen, Natsubayashi-san let her go, but she was too late—Hinami was right where Nanami-san wanted her.

"Hmmm...I wouldn't expect you to say something like that, Aoi," she said, as brightly as ever, but with a hint of a more grown-up kind of mischief. "Poke!"

"Ooh!"

Nanami-san jabbed Hinami lightly in the ribs on her right side, and Hinami responded with a sound so sexy I never would have imagined it from her previous behavior. Nanami-san slowly, teasingly walked her first two fingers up Hinami's side to her armpit and poked three times.

"This is your weak point, isn't it?"

"Heyyy! Mimimi...!"

Hinami clamped both arms down by her sides and pushed away the hand that had started to crawl up again. Nanami-san took the opportunity to move away from Natsubayashi-san and circle around behind Hinami. Then she wrapped her right arm around Hinami's waist and grabbed her left side through the gap between her shirt and skirt. The next thing I knew, she had cupped Hinami's chin with her left hand and was brushing her lips with one finger. At the same time, her left elbow had pinned down Hinami's left arm. She sure had some technique.

"What? Did you say something? Aoi?"

Nanami-san had stopped moving and was whispering a hair's breadth from Hinami's cheek.

"I said sto—eeek!"

As soon as Hinami started to talk, Nanami-san drew a circle with the finger that was resting on her side, and her reply turned into a loud squeal. All the uncool guys in class, including me, stared at her with blank faces.

"What was that? Tell me again."

"Just...leave...me...," Hinami managed to say, bending her still-free right arm at the elbow and sticking it out a little. *Oh, that's what she's up to. Getting ready for an elbow blow.*

"Ooh...♡"

"Eee?!"

In a flash, the left hand that had been stroking Hinami's lip snaked around under her right armpit in a semblance of a hug. Hinami responded by slamming her armpit shut, thereby failing in her attempt at an elbow blow. Nanami-san craned her head around and brought it so close to Hinami's face it looked like she was about to kiss her, but all she said was a satisfied, "Too bad. ♡" She smiled mysteriously...

And then, as if she'd just gotten an idea, Hinami turned her face toward Nanami-san. They stared at each other, glassy-eyed. *Now what's happening?*

Hinami brought her lips toward Nanami-san's. *Huh? Really?* When they were so close I could hardly tell if they were touching or not, she parted them slightly. Nanami-san slowly parted her own lips. Closer and closer, and then...

Foooh!

Hinami blew hard into Nanami-san's mouth. This unexpected attack landed perfectly, and Nanami-san loosened her hold and staggered back a few steps. Pressing her lips with the pad of her finger, she looked at Hinami with a mixture of frustration, enjoyment, and satisfaction. Her cheeks were red.

"…Yup, just like I thought. I'm no match for you, Aoi."

Hinami looked fed up. "Geez, Mimimi, you are so silly! You give up yet?" she scolded in a somewhat childish tone.

"Well, only if 'giving up' means…"

Nanami-san turned her misty eyes up toward the ceiling.

"…That next time I'm not letting you win." She stuck her tongue out clownishly and winked.

"Hey! What she means is, we're not putting up with your sexual harassment anymore!" Natsubayashi-san said, jabbing her finger up toward Nanami-san.

"Ah-ha-ha. You're still in love with Aoi, I see."

"Am not!" Natsubayashi-san turned her face away before continuing. "Thanks for earlier, Minmi." Her voice was suddenly serious, and her eyes completely sincere.

"…What for? I didn't do anything," Nanami-san said.

"Don't give me that! Just let me say thanks!"

"Huh? Sometimes you say complicated stuff… You better not act like that *tama*-rrow!"

Despite Nanami-san's little pun, the conversation seemed to have a deeper meaning. My guess was that Natsubayashi-san was thanking her for acting so cheerful and happy during the exchange with Nakamura. That would make sense—she really did save our butts.

Now that the girl-on-girl action was over, the male spectators wandered away. I thought of doing the same, but then changed my mind and walked over to the three girls. After all, I'd been part of the earlier incident, and I figured Hinami's presence would make talking to them easier. Mostly, though, I wanted to get closer to my goal.

"Um, Hinami…Hinami-san, thanks for that. You really saved me."

Hinami responded with a genuine grin, not one of her salesperson smiles. Honestly, did she have a split personality?

"No problem! You're actually pretty funny, Tomozaki-kun. I was smiling the whole time I was listening to you guys."

I almost laughed at how girly she sounded.

"I just said what I was thinking…"

"I could tell."

"Ah-ha-ha-ha! He's still going!" Next to the smiling Hinami, Nanami-san was cracking up again.

"You laugh too much, Nanami-san," I said.

"Sorry, sorry...oh, and just call me Mimimi!"

"Um..."

"Only teachers ever call her Nanami-san!"

That was Hinami. Basically, she was ordering me to call Nanami-san Mimimi. *Okay, fine then. At least it's not real first-name basis.*

"Um, okay, Mimimi, then."

"Thanks, Tomozaki!"

"What about you, Hanabi?" Hinami asked.

"Whatever."

"Okay...Tama, then?" Hinami suggested.

"Aoi?!" Natsubayashi-san squealed in surprise, looking up at Hinami.

"Ah-ha-ha-ha! Why not? We're all buddies!"

"Um...Tama? Why Tama? Your name's Hanabi Natsubayashi, right?" I asked.

"Well, because Hanabi means fireworks, and when people watch fireworks, they shout 'Tamaya,' right? Also, because it sounds cute!" Nanami-sa—er, Mimimi—explained excitedly.

"Yeah! You don't mind, do you, Tama?" Hinami asked.

"Wait, you're betraying me, too?!" she snapped back.

Once again, Hinami was giving me an order. It was gonna be tough, but then again, not as tough as dropping polite formalities altogether.

"Um, okay, Tama...chan?"

"Ah-ha-ha-ha! When you say it like that, she really does sound like a pet!"

"Stop messing with people's names, Minmi!" Tama-chan scolded.

"Um, so...?" I was confused, but just then Tama-chan jumped in.

"It's fine, just call me Tama-chan... I'm used to it anyway."

She didn't look annoyed. In fact, she was acting oddly sincere. It felt weird when everyone else was joking around, but I don't think she was lying, anyway.

"…Okay, so we'll go with Tama-chan… Thanks." I said.

"You don't have to say 'thank you' all the time!"

"Ha-ha-ha!"

She was a weird one.

The four of us managed to have a little conversation during the one- or two-minute walk to the next class. Of course, Hinami was nudging me along the whole time. If you were wondering, Tama-chan said the reason she calls Mimimi "Minmi" is because Mimimi is just too hard to say.

And that was my crazy first day.

I'd only been waiting in Sewing Room #2 for a couple of minutes when Hinami arrived.

"…Hey," I said.

"Hi. Let's get started."

"Oh, okay."

We were starting on a more solemn note than I'd expected, which made me nervous.

"First, congratulations on accomplishing your mission."

Oh, a compliment from the boss.

"Th-thanks."

"Technically speaking it's not clear if you talked to them or they talked to you, but since you talked to four girls instead of the three that were required, I'll let it slide."

"Well, that's a relief. I was worried if it counted."

The truth was, of those four, I'd only initiated with one.

"So how was it? What are your impressions?"

"My impressions?"

"Anything is fine. What do you remember most clearly?"

"That's hard. There's so much…"

I scratched my head.

"But I guess the thing I remember most…was in the home-ec room… The thing about *Atafami*."

"What thing about *Atafami*?"

"Yeah, you said Nakamura had lost at *Atafami* in front of everybody."

"Oh, that," Hinami said, smiling.

"And you made it into a joke. That surprised me."

"Okay, but this is a time for *self*-reflection. The focus is supposed to be on what *you* did, not me…"

"Oh right."

"It's fine. I had to do it, either way."

"How so?"

"He seemed like he had a pretty strong grudge against you for beating him. Like he didn't want to mention it, or like it was his dark past… You must have really crushed him, huh?"

"Well, yeah… He didn't take a single stock from me."

"That's what I thought," she said with another smirk.

"Was that bad?"

"Not particularly. But it was bad that everyone was tiptoeing around it. Because of that, all his regret over losing got bottled up inside him. Then when no one could mention it at school, that made it awkward, too, and I'm sure he had all kinds of other feelings that couldn't be released."

"So that's what was going on."

"Yeah. And the more time passed, the more those negative feelings built up until he was like a balloon ready to pop. And the harder it got for anyone to mention it. Well, that's my take on it, at least."

"Makes sense."

"Once things got to that point, Nakamura went harder and harder on you, and the balloon became trickier and trickier to pop. Since Nakamura is an influential member of the class, his rudeness to you destabilized your position. That would spell trouble if you want to be successful in the real world, and that's why it was necessary to prick the balloon as soon as possible and just blow it up."

"Blow it up."

"Yeah. Just give it a little prick by saying something in front of everyone and turning it into a joke."

Turn it into a joke… She made it sound so simple.

"It wasn't that easy, was it?"

"Well, it wasn't that hard in terms of technique, but I doubt anyone but me could have done it." She smiled broadly. "No one else is brave enough."

"O-okay." *This girl is a force to be reckoned with.*

"So that's what I did. I think Nakamura will ease up a little now, too."

I would never have guessed that so much thought went into that little stunt.

"Back on topic. What do you remember most about what you did today?"

Hmm, what I did...

"Probably how tactless I was in conversations."

"Tactless how?"

"It's hard to explain. Like, saying the right thing to keep things fun for people."

"I see... But everyone seemed to be having fun in home ec. I was surprised."

"Uh...that was different."

"Different?"

"I was just saying whatever came into my head, and they happened to think it was funny. We weren't really communicating."

"If you said what you were thinking, isn't that communication?" She was studying me.

"I guess."

"You're misunderstanding something."

"What?"

"Okay. Conversation is essentially telling another person what you're thinking."

"Um, but...wouldn't both people end up pushing their opinions on each other?"

Conversation was supposed to be about respecting each other's opinions and empathizing, right? Like Mimimi did.

"Not at all. You're thinking that conversation just means getting the other person's ideas and sympathizing or empathizing with them, but that's not the heart of it."

Just like she said, I did think conversation was the same as sympathizing or empathizing. After all, everyone did that—both adults out in the world and my own classmates. At least, that's how it looked to me. And since I was bad at it, I always felt uncomfortable.

"It's not?"

"Nope. Clearly, it would be arrogant to ignore what the other person said and then say some entirely unrelated thought of your own. But that's not what you did, is it?"

Ummm... "I didn't?"

"No. You explained it. You listened to what Mimimi said, and it made you think about how young people these days have amazing powers of empathy. So you said that. Which means you listened to what she said and had a related thought of your own. In which case, you weren't being arrogant."

"Uh, I guess so?"

"It's true that simply sympathizing with what someone says often does smooth out the interaction. But listen. People have surprisingly sharp intuition. Eventually, they'll figure out what you're doing. In the long run, people trust those who don't simply sympathize with what they say, but instead pause to think for themselves and then say what they came up with. You did that. A lot of people can't, and they suffer for it."

"I—I see."

I kinda got it, but kinda didn't.

"So as far as that goes, you did extremely well for a first-timer in today's field practice."

Really? "Extremely well" was great news.

"But you did horribly in other areas. Nothing positive whatsoever. The thing with Kikuchi-san was awful. You asked her to lend you some tissues, and when she did, you were still smiling under your mask, and *then* you pretended to blow your nose. You should be sinking into the floor with shame."

"Hinami... If you're using the good-cop, bad-cop method, your bad cop is a little too strong..."

"I could see that."

Like I said, not many young people seemed to act that way these days.

"She especially doesn't get along with people like Nakamura who tend to control the tone of a conversation."

Aha.

"Makes sense."

"They've gotten into little…conflicts many times. Hanabi's gotten burned in the past, and she feels responsible. On the other hand, a guy like Nakamura is obviously gonna think Hanabi should stop being so stubborn and just go with the program for once in her life. It has more to do with his own pride and stubbornness rather than malice, though… At least, that's how it looks to me."

"Hmm. If that's the case…it sounds annoying."

"Exactly! If I'm around, I can smooth things over like I did today, but no one else can handle Nakamura the way I can. Hanabi could be traumatized again when I'm not watching. But I can't follow her around everywhere she goes! …So it's a tough situation."

Hanami's emotions were slipping in and out of her voice, which was unusual for her.

"…So even Aoi Hinami feels helpless sometimes. I thought you could do anything," I commented nonchalantly.

"I can't do *any*thing," she mumbled with that same sorrowful expression I'd seen once before.

"Huh?"

"…Is that what you were expecting? There's *nothing* I can't do. I'll show you one of these days that I can even fix the situation with Hanabi."

"R-really?"

She was back to her usual confident self… Was she joking? What a waste of acting talent.

"But, I don't think T-Tama-chan would listen if you told her to behave herself…"

"Right… Plus, I wouldn't want her to. It's rare for someone to wear their heart on their sleeve the way she does."

"Yeah, she's pretty unique."

"Hanabi's heart is always laid bare, which means it's poorly defended. Someone has to act as her armor. Someone has to come swooping and fend off the attacks, or else her heart will get all torn up... Anyway, that's the story with Hanabi."

"Huh."

I was nodding admiringly when Hinami caught me off guard with her next comment.

"That's why I think you two might have surprisingly good chemistry."

"Huh? Really? Why?"

"...Never mind. For now, just spend the evening thinking back on what happened today and what you learned as well as you can. You won't develop very quickly if you're just following my instructions all the time. You have to believe in it yourself. Okay?"

"Uh, um, okay."

"We good for today?"

"Uh-huh."

Hinami gestured for me to leave Sewing Room #2. She'd head home a couple minutes later. I obeyed without protest...and only realized once I'd left that a normie would have said, "Ladies first." I still had a long way to go.

* * *

I was lying on my bed, just starting to fall asleep. She'd told me to reflect on the day as well as I could, but where should I start? Honestly speaking, my experience points were extremely low when it came to relationships. If someone asked me to come up with an analysis of today's events that went beyond Hinami's, I couldn't do much more than turn tail and run.

Anyway, in terms of my own feelings about the day, I was surprised by the power of that invisible monster on the battlefield of group dynamics: "the mood." I had no clue how to fight that monster, or even if the word "fight" was the right one for this situation. All I knew was that the battle-field belonged to the wild-animal trainers—the people like Hinami and Nakamura who were good at taming the invisible mood monster.

I had a mental image of Hinami and Nakumura facing each other in an oval coliseum, trying to parry an enormous deformed monster in the center with their chosen weapon and ultimately lead it to devour their opponent. Nakamura had a whip, Hinami a cape. Neither laid a hand on the other directly; in the end it was the mood that would kill them. Could I join that battle? I sure couldn't picture myself there. I drifted off to sleep thinking about all of this.

By the way, Hinami had texted me a very impersonal *"7 PM, first to take five matches wins,"* which led us to a set of friend matches. I won five in a row. She still had a long way to go herself.

3

Hunting solo nets you a surprising number of experience points

"Starting today, we're going to correct your posture."

Thus began Hinami's instructions the following morning.

"Posture?"

"Yes, your posture. Do you remember what I said? The three keys to appearance are expression, build, and posture."

"Yeah, I remember." She'd mentioned that when we were in her room.

"Once you have those three covered, you'll have the foundation. You've got an average build, so as long as you fix your expression and your posture, you'll have enough points to pass. We're working on your expression with the mask training, so that just leaves posture."

My goal was surprisingly close.

"But how do I fix that? Is it even that bad to start with?"

"Well, it's not great…but more importantly, most people have poor posture."

"Really? So you're saying that if I have good posture, I'll look especially good?"

"Half right, half wrong."

"Half?"

"There are different kinds of bad posture."

She bent her elbows, bowed her legs, tilted her chin up, and walked forward swinging her shoulders.

"This is one kind of bad posture, but it's an intimidating one. It's not the best, but it's common among normies."

"You look like a thug. I get the feeling you're strong."

"Right. Then there's this one…"

She rounded her back, stuck her neck forward, drew her shoulders in, and started walking again.

"This is also a kind of bad posture. But this one makes you look weak, doesn't it?"

"Yeah. Like a geek or an artsy type."

I would have assumed she was bad at sports. Posture really did make a big difference. *She sure is good at impressions.*

"So you see, most people have poor posture, but people further down the social ladder usually have the weak type."

"Really? Why's that?"

"Well, I can think of a lot of reasons. For one, they tend to spend a lot of time on the computer or playing video games, which tends to create that kind of posture."

"Makes sense."

"But I don't think that's the main reason. It's an issue of body and soul."

"Body and soul?"

"Yeah. Try puffing your chest out and putting both hands on your hips, like you're saying 'ahem.'"

"L-like this?" I tried to look imposing.

"...How do you feel? Just by changing your posture, don't you have more of a presence?"

"Yeah, I do."

She was right. By striking that pose, I felt a little more confident, a little more like, *Hey, you can't tell me what to be.*

"But couldn't I be feeling that way because you suggested it to me?"

"That could be part of it, but your body and heart are closely connected. Think about when you feel nervous and cross your arms, or how spread your legs and let the tension out of your shoulders because you're relaxed. Or the reverse, like that famous line about how if you smile even when you're sad, the sadness itself will go away."

"Yeah, I guess I've heard that."

"If you stand proud with your body, your heart will stand proud, too. And if your heart is feeling down, your body will slump. It's not a question of which one comes first—they're a set. Normies have the heart for it, and their posture naturally reflects that."

"Okay, I get that."

"So…"

Hinami started walking forward in a way that showed off her figure yet wasn't intimidating and at the same time projected an aura of mature confidence.

"You don't have to make your posture this good. I mean, this isn't something you can do overnight. You've got to spend a long time adjusting your pelvis and retraining your muscles to achieve this. You don't have that kind of time. Plus, it's not necessary."

Wow. She really could do anything. "So what should I do?"

"Just stop looking so weak." She pointed at my chest.

"…How?"

"There's an easy fix… Come over here."

"Huh?" I questioned, following her all the same.

"Put your back and shoulders against the wall. Heels together, toes straight forward."

I did what she said.

"Do you feel the tension in your glutes?"

"Huh? Oh, uh, yeah. I really do."

Standing like this really had made my butt tighter—and as I was thinking about it, Hinami came up to me with purpose. *Uh-oh, what's going on?* Her near-perfect symmetrical features were right up next to my face, and since the wall was behind me I couldn't back away. Was the classy, clean scent I noticed coming from her shampoo?

She slowly reached her hands toward me.

"Yes, very good," she said, touching my butt.

"Aaaah! Wh-wh-what are you doing?"

"Checking. I just touched your butt a little; don't get so worked up. You're a guy, right?"

"That's not the point!"

Seriously, stop! You're gonna give me a heart attack! I'm already overheating!

"…What's with that look on your face? Anyway, you're really doing well. Keep the tension in your butt and move your toes and heels back to a normal position. Now press your shoulders and hips against the wall. Don't release your butt."

She kept giving me instructions like she hadn't just copped a feel, and I scrambled to obey.

"Like this?"

"Yes... Can you tell the difference? You look more imposing already."

...*Hey, she's right.* I hadn't noticed. "Yeah, I do."

"Now step away from the wall... Your posture doesn't look weak anymore. Nope, definitely not," she said, giving me a once-over from a slight distance. *Seriously?*

"This is a little harder than it seemed at first."

"Yeah. You're using muscles you don't usually use. But from now on, whenever you're standing, I want you to stand like this. Even when you're sitting you should stick out your chest and tense your butt muscles, if you can. Most people with posture like yours generally don't open their chests, and they have saggy butts. I want you make a habit of always keeping your chest open and your butt taut."

"'Always' again, huh?"

"Obviously. This is your character creation. You're trying to find a way to improve your base stats. If it's not a constant baseline, you can't call it a basic ability, can you?"

Fair enough. "I understand. That can't be all I have to do today...can it?"

"Of course not. There's one more thing."

Yeah, I knew it. She wouldn't let me off that easy.

"What?"

"This isn't a very hard one. All you have to do is talk to me and someone I'm with, like Mimimi or Hanabi or another friend."

That's all? At least she made it sound easy.

"Well, I bet it'll be a cinch compared to yesterday's assignment, since you'll be there."

"Right. That's your assignment through Friday."

"So the next four days."

"Yeah."

That's a fair length of time. Got it. "And what am I going to learn from this?"

If I didn't understand the why, the learning process wouldn't be very efficient.

"Wow, you're getting very proactive. That's a good habit to get into."

"Thanks."

"Anyway, it's simple. You're collecting experience points."

"Collecting experience points?"

"Yeah. Happens all the time, right? Like when you have really a strong character in your party in the early stages of an RPG and fight a powerful enemy together. Then they break away from the party, and at the end of the game they turn out to be really important and rejoin you. At that point, the main characters are around the same level, and you think to yourself, 'Wow, I really grew a lot.' Y'know what I mean?"

She seemed so happy whenever she talked about gaming.

"Oh yeah, I know what you're talking about. I always wonder why the other guy hasn't leveled up, too."

"Exactly!" Hinami replied excitedly, then coughed. "Anyway, same thing. I'm gonna be a temporary party member to help you fight a powerful enemy and net you some EXP."

"Okay, I get it."

So I'd be raising my level with a handicap.

"And you'll be collecting information at the same time. In RPGs, if you fight a boss once, you learn their moveset so you know what to do the next time you fight them, right? You know their weaknesses and how much damage they do. Which means you know how to attack them and when to recover, right?"

"Right."

"You'll be doing something similar. I want you to pick up the technique by observing the flow of real conversations."

Just "pick it up," huh? I felt like in my current state, I'd probably just be watching the conversation go by without catching much of anything.

"Is it enough to just watch and learn? Is there nothing in particular I should be watching for?"

Hinami thought for a moment. "Good question…You'll probably have conversations with around twenty people in the next four days. Just analyze those conversations in general terms."

"Analyze?" *Actually, twenty is an awfully big number.*

"Yes. Think about how to choose topics or close the distance, things like that. I want you to do your best to think about each conversational technique."

"Okay… Analyze."

I didn't know if I could do it, but I figured I'd give it a whirl.

"Also…I don't think I'll be very good at jumping into conversations with people I don't know. What do you suggest?"

"Oh, you don't need to jump in."

"Huh?"

"The goal right now is observation. Don't worry, I'll make sure there's a good reason for you to be there. You just focus on observing."

Just leave it to her, then…? I guess?

"That's about it for now. I'll come get you after school, so study or something while you wait."

"After school? What are we doing after school?"

"I'm gonna walk to the train station with Mimimi and Hanabi and a couple of guys, and you're going with us."

"What?!"

This wasn't a bit of light conversation—it was full-on going home together.

* * *

"Yeah. You didn't know, Mimimi?"

"No. What, did everyone else?"

"Uh-huh, we totally did."

"Well, you *would* know, Aoi."

"I knew, too."

We were about to head home after school. The group was talking excitedly about the killer drawing on the blackboard at the back of the classroom, which had actually been done by one of the guys in the group, Daichi Matsumoto, and another guy named Kiyu Hashiguchi.

"What about you, Tomozaki-kun?"

Hinami had been periodically tossing me opportunities to join the conversation.

"Um, I've seen him drawing before, so I knew."

"What! Tomozaki-kun knew and I didn't?!"

"That was rude! Ha-ha!"

Then after she'd opened a little space for me, someone else would say something. That was the general pattern. Hinami would bump the ball to me, and I would try keep it aloft in the safest possible way, trying at least to not demolish her attempts to help me. As long as the ball didn't hit the ground, Hinami was able to catch it from whatever crazy angle I'd sent it from and tip it over to the other team's side of the court.

As a result, my conversational observation was proceeding smoothly. Except, given that I was a rank beginner, I probably wasn't making many meaningful observations.

"...Right? I'm so exhausted."

"You said that yesterday, too, Daichi."

"Yeah, I've been doing some lifting."

"Wow!"

Now the guys were talking about working out, and Mimimi was chiming in. She was impressive. She both brought up topics of her own and expanded on other people's topics, and she smiled the whole time, which kept the mood lively. She must be a naturally cheerful person. I needed to steal some of her tricks. Introducing new topics was beyond me, so I figured I should focus on expanding on existing ones.

"What area are you focusing on?" she asked.

"Pretty much my whole body. I do my arms, my pecs, my abs, my back, and my legs."

"Dang."

"Oh hey..." Without warning, I jumped into the conversation. It was now or never! Hinami's eyebrows shot up in surprise as she glanced at me.

What? Did I screw up? But it was too late to turn back. All I could do was give it a try.

"Are you working on your butt, too?"

The mood after that comment was best described as: *Butt?*

* * *

"I'm really sorry about yesterday!"

It was the next morning in Sewing Room #2. The instant I saw Hinami's face, I apologized.

"...Are you talking about the butt incident?"

"Yes. I'm so sorry for speaking out of turn and making everything weird!" I said, thinking that anything called "the butt incident" was kind of impressive, even as I apologized sincerely for a second time.

After I'd made the comment the day before, Daichi Matsumoto replied, with some confusion, that he thought you couldn't tone your butt muscles. Just as everyone was starting to wonder awkwardly if it was some kind of joke, Hinami stepped in and averted disaster by nonchalantly saying that she worked *her* butt muscles. The conversation veered toward the question of whether butt workouts were the secret to her attractive physique. After that, I stayed quiet.

"Really, I just went and..."

"You don't have to say the same thing over and over. I'm not worried about it anyway."

"Huh?"

"You were thinking for yourself and taking action, right? Okay, you floundered some, but I'm not going to criticize you for trying."

"Hi...Hinami..."

She was so forgiving...

"What's important is your assignment. If you were focusing on your misstep to the point that you didn't actually do what I wanted you to, *then* I would be mad."

"Oh right. You mean reflecting and analyzing the day's events as well as I could, right? I basically did that."

"Then we're all good. You still have three days left, so you can tell me about all your conclusions at the end. I think we're done for today."

"Uh, wait a second."

"What? Did you not understand something?"

"No, it's more like…something happened that I didn't understand. Actually, yesterday on the way home from school…"

"…What?" Hinami asked warily.

Glancing at her, I started describing what had happened.

* * *

"Bye!" "Bye!" "See you tomorrow!"

The six of us had arrived at the station after leaving school and were getting ready to board our various trains.

"Oh, here's my train."

"Oh, me too! See you!"

"Bye-bye!"

"Later!"

The group started to break up. Hinami disappeared on the train that had just arrived, heading in the opposite direction from my house. Which meant I had to keep talking to the people going in the same direction as me, without her help.

She'd considered that, too, of course. She'd told me I should be okay since the ride was only ten minutes or so, and I'd be with Mimimi and Daichi, who probably would keep the conversation going. Both of them would be getting off at different stops from mine; plus, it was Mimimi. Hinami acted like knowing what stop everyone got off at was totally natural; it was unnerving, but also reassuring.

The train came and we got on. Just like she'd promised, the two of them chatted like they were born for it, so the conversation on the train went okay. Mimimi asked me questions now and then, which I barely managed to answer with some boring comment, and then she would find something funny about what I said and laugh. But, like that time in home ec, I didn't feel like she was making fun of me. She seemed as good at conversations as Hinami was.

We got to my station, and I congratulated myself silently on one mission cleared.

"Oh, this is my stop, so I'll see you guys later," I said.

"Really? Me too! I'll walk home with you!" Mimimi chirped.

"Huh?!"

The same stop? Wait a second, Hinami, what's going on?

"Hey, Tomozaki, don't try anything funny!" Matsumoto warned.

Wait a second! I'm already embarrassed; why is he suddenly making mean jokes?

"N-no, I wouldn't d-do that!"

"Ooh, he's panicking…! What if my chastity is in danger?!"

"Ah-ha-ha-ha! Anyway, you're blocking the door. See ya!"

Mimimi and I got off the train together.

"Mimimi, is this really your stop…?"

The doors closed.

"…It is, isn't it…?"

"Yeah, why?"

"Oh, no reason…"

* * *

"So her stop and mine weren't different, were they?" I asked Hinami.

Apparently, I wasn't making sense to her. "Mimimi gets off at Kitayono. And you get off at Omiya, right? That's a different stop…"

"My stop's Kitayono!"

"What…?"

She sank into thought for a minute, then looked up with realization.

"…You were trying to be thoughtful, weren't you? But you didn't have to. That slipped past me. Rookie mistake…"

"What are you talking about?"

"When nanashi and NO NAME met offline, you were supposed to go to the station closest to your house!"

"…Oh…"

That explained it. Instead of telling her the station that was actually closest to me, I'd tried to be considerate by telling her to go to the terminal because it was easier to get to. But she didn't know that...

"Well, no use for regret. Water under the bridge, okay? ...Anyway, what happened after that?"

"Oh right..."

At her prompt, I continued my story.

* * *

We headed out of the station and started down the street. I was so nervous even my gait felt awkward.

"This is the first chance we've had to talk alone, isn't it?! I mean, we just started talking at all the other day!"

Mimimi giggled and slapped her forehead.

"Y-yeah."

"What are you so nervous about?! Be confident!"

She slapped my back quite a bit harder than most people would consider appropriate.

"Ow! That stung!"

"Really?" She cackled cheerfully, apparently even more cheerful than usual. I think that was her version of being thoughtful toward me.

"Y-you sure have a lot of energy, Mimimi..."

"Right? My plan is to get through life on my cheerfulness and smiles."

"Ha-ha, that's amazing...I mean, that sounds hard..."

"Hard how?" She peered at my face curiously.

"I mean...surely there are times in life when you can't be cheerful and smiley...right?"

Mimimi blinked. "What are you talking about?! The harder things get, the more you smile! Frowning just makes it harder, right?"

"Oh."

Hinami had said the same thing. Something about your body and heart being connected.

"Yeah, I've heard that. Like, if you stand up straight and smile, you'll feel better."

"Yeah, exactly! I think life will be more fun if I'm sunny and cheerful all the time!"

That was an amazingly positive attitude. But at the same time…how do I put this? Why does every day need to be fun? Okay, in my case you'd expect every day to be *not* fun, which may have numbed my capacity for enjoyment in general, but I wanted to say that human beings can have a lot of not-especially-fun moments and still be fine. *It's like…protecting your own world is more important, I guess.*

While I was thinking about this, silence stretched on. Was it my turn to talk? Yup, it sure was.

"You don't agree? Well, everybody's different," Mimimi remarked.

"Oh sorry. Y-yeah."

For a minute, things got awkward. *Aaah! I'm sorry!* Since I'd clammed up, Mimimi had offered a comment of her own, but then I'd gone and given her an answer that went nowhere. This is what happens when you have no communication skills!

"Hey, anyway! Can I ask you something I've been wondering about?"

Mimimi smiled as if to say, *No worries, you didn't mess up.* Like I said, she's incredible.

"Huh? What?"

Mimimi made her hand like a mask and brought it toward my mouth.

"Be honest with me, Tomozaki! Is something going on between you and Aoi?"

I sputtered and coughed, choking on my words.

"Aha! Just as I thought! Something *is* going on. What is it, what is it?! Come on, I'm like your big sister! You can tell me! Well?"

"There's nothing going on!"

"Are you suuure? I swear I saw you two giving each other fishy glances! And the other day, you almost forgot to use 'san' with Aoi's name, but not with anyone else!"

…I did? Even if I had, did people normally notice that sort of thing? Normies make you think they're just cheerful, but in reality, they're masters of reading the room and sussing out people's emotions. One false

move and I was done for. If she already knew this much, a clumsy attempt at a cover-up wouldn't save me.

"Nothing's up! I mean, we're not enemies or anything like that, but Hinami is friends with everyone, isn't she?"

"There! You did it again! You didn't use 'san.' Just as I thought, very suspicious. Tomozaki! Why did you try to hide it? A guilty conscience, perhaps? Tell me everything! Spill!"

"I told you, nothing's going on! Anyway, you think Aoi Hinami, the school idol, would do anything with me to feel guilty about? No way!"

"Got me there!"

"Hey!" I shot back teasingly.

"Ha-ha-ha-ha! I like that! You really are funny sometimes, Tomozaki!"

"Gimme a break! I wasn't trying to be funny, and come on, that 'some-times' was unnecessary."

Somehow, I didn't feel so nervous anymore. I probably had Mimimi's conversation style to thank for that. Or maybe it was just that we were talking about a certain rude gamer.

"See, you should be happy like that all the time. You're always so glum."

"That's none of your business… But actually, I'm fine with not being happy all the time."

"…Really?! What do you mean by that?"

She really latched on to that. What am I supposed to say now? "Um, how do I explain this? Being fun and happy isn't always the right answer…maybe?"

"Huh! You're the first person I've ever heard say that! Gimme the deets! The 411!"

"41…?"

Oh right, 411. Who actually says that? "It's hard to explain. For example, I like *Atafami* and other games, and…"

"Yeah, I've heard you're super-good, too! And, and?"

"Yeah, um… it's not at all like fun stuff at school. But I still spend my time playing *Atafami*, I mean…"

"Hmm. But isn't *Atafami* fun?"

"Um…I mean, it is, definitely, but it's like… I don't play *Atafami* because I want to have fun. I like *Atafami* and I work hard at it, so the fun comes as a kind of side effect... Sorry I can't explain it better..."

"No, I get it."

"Really?"

"Yeah, actually... I think you're a little like Tama in that sense."

"...Like Tama-chan?"

I couldn't see that at all... But Hinami had said something similar.

"I guess...she doesn't bend, or she doesn't let herself be bent, ha-ha, and that's a really good thing. Anyway, she's got that side to her."

"Yeah, I can see that."

"You can tell? For example, even if bending would make a situation more enjoyable, she won't do it unless she thinks it's right. She's really extreme. I've gotta give her props for that."

"That's unusual among our generation, isn't it?"

"Ha-ha-ha! Here comes Mr. Talk-Show Host again!"

"Shut up!"

"Ah-ha-ha! ...Anyway, I think that side of her is amazing, but I also know I don't have it in me. I mean, I'm bent over backward most of the time! I bend every which way and do whatever it takes to make things fun. I'm bent so far over I can hear my back popping!"

"R-really?" I'd thought it was a natural gift.

"Oh, definitely. I'm a young maiden with many worries...I mean, is there anyone that doesn't have any? Compared to Tama, my worries are tiny!"

"She really does seem...to have a lot of problems."

"Right? I totally agree. But that's why someone more flexible like me has to protect her. That's the situation! So! What do you think? You gonna cry for me? Or pat my back?"

She stood in front of me with her hands outspread.

"I see," I said. I'd been lost in thought, so I missed most of what she said. "But how do *you* feel? I mean, I can't imagine you'd enjoy having to keep the mood up all the time."

"Huh? Are you spacing out? But anyway, me? I don't mind! The reason I do it is so things will be more fun, so obviously it's fun! Of course, there are times when I don't want to bend, but what can I do? Life's not perfect! The reason I give in is because it would be worse if I didn't! I'm always trying to go where the fun is!"

"...Okay, I get it. You do what you're best at."

"Exactly! You're full of good lines, aren't you, Tomozaki? My job is bending, and Tama's job is not bending! That's how we function!"

"And you support each other."

"Right, right, exactly! We support each other! You really do know how to sum it up, Tomozaki! Of course, if I had to say one way or the other, I'd say I'm the one who supports Tama, to be accurate. And I'm okay with that!"

She gave another little *ta-ha*.

"Well, to me..."

"Oh, I'm heading this way now! Were you about to say something?"

"No, nothing important."

"Really? Okay, well, see you later, Tomozaki!"

"Uh, yeah, see you."

She waved exaggeratedly and disappeared like a passing storm. I'd started to say something and hadn't finished, but maybe that was okay. It was just my own unsolicited opinion, or rather guess, and it was probably better to keep to myself.

I was going to say that to me, Mimimi seemed like the one being supported.

* * *

"Huh. Nice work," Hinami said flatly.

"Well, Mimimi just kept the energy high while we were talking about serious stuff. The stuff even I can manage."

"That's true, but...it shows that you have a strength."

"...I...do?" What did she mean?

"You did it in home ec, too. Apparently, you're good at saying what's on your mind."

"Uh, saying what's on my mind? Isn't everyone good at that? I mean, all you have to do is say it."

Hinami wagged her finger. "Not quite. There are more people who can't do it than can."

"Huh?"

"For example, Mimimi. Her strength is her flexibility. Do you think she's good at saying what she's thinking?"

"…Oh, I see. You mean she's good at agreeing with the people around her."

"Right," Hinami said, nodding. "What about Hanabi? She's probably good at it, right? At speaking her mind, I mean."

"…Yeah, probably."

"Are there a lot of people like her? Or not so many?"

Uh…not many. Fine, you got me. "So…this is a rare skill I have?"

"Yup. In a sense, this is your weapon, your strong point, your killer technique. And fighting on the field where you're strongest is the foundation of gaming, right?"

"Um, yeah."

"Okay. So if you get in trouble, you can fall back on this skill. Remember that."

"I will."

"Well, there weren't any major problems in the incident you just described, so I'll continue. Consider yourself lucky with the extra EXP… Anyway, keep observing conversations. You all prepared?"

"How can I prepare? …Don't you just head out to the field for this stuff?"

"I think you know the answer. And put some spirit into it. I'm expecting your analysis on the final day."

With that, I headed out to start my three-day exercise in raising my level and gathering information.

Wednesday, lunchtime in the cafeteria.

"Did you catch the last episode yesterday? I wonder what they're gonna do in the finale."

"Yeah, but the part when he was like 'Come back to me!' was so bad. I was laughing the whole time."

"Ha-ha-ha! Me too! That was terrible!"

"Hey look at Tomozaki, he's acting all nervous. He hasn't said anything!"

"Yeah, I know. Weirdo!"

…Hmm, hmm.

Thursday, walking to the station after school.

"Oh, that reminds me, Yukako, was everything okay yesterday? Your dad kept calling you!"

"Oh, that! My brother was actually the one who didn't get it!"

"The little guy?"

"Yeah! When I opened the front door, he was standing there like a statue, and he goes 'Damn it!'"

"What a weirdo!"

"Sounds like something you'd do, Tomozaki!"

"Ha-ha-ha, yeah right."

…Uh-huh.

Friday, between classes.

"Tell us something funny, Takahiro!"

"Hey, don't put me on the spot!"

"Come on!"

"Um…well…yesterday, my girlfriend…"

"Stop showing off!"

"I'm not!"

"Tomozaki, do you have any…never mind, you wouldn't."

"Ha-ha-ha! That was rude!"

…Indeed.

That's pretty much how things went.

"So how was it?"

It was our Friday after-school meeting. For the past four days, I'd been tossed into groups of kids I wasn't particularly close with and forced to observe them, even participate a tiny bit. Four days in the depths of hell. And today we were going over it all.

"My soul is dead."

"…Well, that's the fate of antisocial people. But once you get your expression and posture and conversational skills in shape, you'll be released from that fate soon enough."

"…Are you sure?"

"I don't think you can avoid being insulted. Groups are like that. Once five or six people get together, well…someone's gonna be the sacrifice."

"…I see."

"What matters is your analysis."

"Um, I thought about a lot of stuff, but…"

"Yes?"

The ultimate normie is asking me, the communication-disabled, for the observations I barely managed to scrape together. Of course I'm nervous.

What I noticed was the division of roles in conversations.

It seems to me that each participant in a given conversation has a role to take care of. There are three main ones: the person who introduces new topics, the person who expands on existing topics, and the person who reacts.

For example, on Monday, I observed a conversation that started like this:

"Hey, listen to this! Yesterday at cram school…"

Mimimi always starts by saying something like "Listen to this" or "That reminds me" or "So yesterday…" After that, she mentions something that's not really related to what everyone had been talking about up to that point. Conversations are started by these "introducers." That's obvious enough.

Then there are people who add to the topics with comments like "And then this happened" or "That's similar to this other thing." These are the "expanders."

Finally, you have the people who keep it fun by listening and agreeing or laughing, or occasionally expressing an opinion. These are the "reactors."

Once a given topic has been wrapped up, an introducer will throw out a new topic.

Of course, expanders and reactors sometimes introduce new topics, and introducers take on the role of listener. But it seems to me that the roles are fairly fixed within each group.

And that wasn't all I noticed. Also from Monday:

"Wow, the teacher definitely must have done that on purpose."

"I thought so, too!"

"I bet he likes you, Minmi."

"No way! It's probably the opposite!"

In this case, Kyoya Hashiguchi and Tama-chan were acting as expanders. Even though they were part of the conversation the whole time, I could tell they weren't at the center of it.

"Speaking of, have you memorized the vocab yet? I can't believe we have to remember a hundred words all at once."

This was something a certain key normie said on Wednesday.

What struck me as important was that while everyone in the conversation did quite a bit of expanding, it was almost always the same ones who introduced new topics. On Monday it was Daichi Matsumoto, Mimimi, and Hinami. I almost never observed Tama-chan or Kyoya Hashiguchi introduce a topic. Maybe if I watched for a really long time, I'd see one of them do it, but it was clearly rare. Which suggests that if you don't introduce new topics, you'll never be at the center of things.

Anyway, I couldn't put a specific name on the idea if you asked me to, but that's what I noticed.

"...And since Tama-chan and Kyoya didn't introduce any new topics, they didn't control the mood. That's about it."

Hinami nodded.

"Hmm. If the average person listened to what you just said, they'd probably be like, *And? Does that mean something?* In other words, everything you said is completely obvious."

Her words hit home extra hard because I'd been wondering that myself.

"…But for people like you and me who are assessing the situation with a focus on cause and effect, it's an important observation. Worthy of nanashi, I'd say."

Just as I was reeling from the damage of her previous comment, she praised me. I was happy, unsurprisingly. She had me completely under the control of her good cop bad cop routine.

"R-really?"

"Yeah. You understand now, right? What are the two things you need in order to be good at conversation?"

…Oh, okay. I do get it.

"Improving my ability to introduce and expand on topics?"

"Hexactly."

"Huh?"

"All that's left is to figure out how to improve those abilities."

"Wait, wait, wait. This is the third time you've said that 'Hexactly' thing. What *is* that?"

"…"

No response!

"…Okay fine, I give up. It's a habit, and sometimes I slip up and say it. You don't recognize it? It's what Oinko always said in that retro game *Go Go Oinko*. I loved that game when I was a kid. To tell you the truth, I try not to say it because it's embarrassing, but I'm tired of avoiding it. It always slips out, whether I like it or not, so from now on I'm gonna say it all the time. Just ignore it, okay? Story over."

What's with this girl? She gives a big speech, then suddenly gets all defensive and ends the conversation.

Wait a sec…

"…Oinko! I thought I recognized that phrase from somewhere! I remember now! You like that game?"

"…Wow. I should have expected the top gamer in Japan to remember that one. Hardly anyone knows about it. Which is weird because it was super-famous back in the day!" For once, Hinami sounded excited.

"Totally! I used to play it at a friend's house when I was a kid. Oinko the pig was super-cute. He always said, 'That's so correct, I think I've been hexed!' ...That was a good game."

"Yeah, it was. They made you think it was just gonna be another crappy manga spinoff, but it actually had stuff you wouldn't expect from the technology back then, like 2.5-D parallax scrolling. Just technically speaking, it was amazing! But at the same time, it was one of those unique little worlds kids love. The characters were so cute! Seriously good game."

Hinami was smiling like an innocent little girl. *I—I didn't even know she could make that expression.*

"I'm with you there," I said, looking away from her.

"I should've known you'd get it! When it comes to games, Oinko was like my...I mean..." Hinami turned her face away and coughed, like she'd suddenly realized something. "We're way off topic."

Maybe because she'd been rambling enthusiastically about something she liked, her cheeks were flushed.

"Oh yeah. Um..."

"We were talking about how to be good at conversations, right?" Hinami said, sounding disappointed. She crossed her arms with some discontent.

"Right. And we can talk about Oinko another time."

"Yeah. Let's get back to the point. So...do you know how to develop that skill?"

"Um...by imitating people who are good at it?"

"Hexactly."

"There it is."

"Once you've figured out what the two important skills are, you just watch the best and copy them. And now that you know what's important, you know what to pay attention to, right?"

"Sounds good to me."

"By the way, you mentioned the 'mood' earlier. Do you know what that is?"

"Uh, mood?"

…Now that she mentioned it, I realized I'd been thinking in vague terms, like "that person commands the mood" or "the mood is getting weird in this conversation," but if someone asked me to define it, I wouldn't be able to.

"No, I don't. What is it?"

Might as well ask the expert.

"So 'mood' refers to the standards for right and wrong in a particular situation."

Um, the standards for right and wrong? "What do you mean?"

"If I break it down, it's the standard for what you should and shouldn't do. Within a specific group, that is. For example, in some groups, you'll earn praise for being easy-going and upbeat, but others, like, say, a group of college students, might dislike that and think it's childish or uncool. That standard for good and bad is what people call the 'mood.'"

"Hmm."

I felt like I was starting to get the idea. If I said Mimimi was easily influenced by the mood and Tama-chan wasn't influenced by it at all, that would make sense.

"The 'mood' refers to these standards for right and wrong, or good and bad. Specifically when they hold true within a particular group and not anywhere else."

Hmm. "I get the gist, but I'm not sure that explanation's enough."

"That's fine. We're getting into the weeds here, which is not necessary at your level. Just keep it in mind as something that might come in handy in the future. For now, it's enough to have a vague sense of it as 'mood.'"

"That's enough? …Okay. But there's something essential I still haven't asked you."

Hinami grinned. "And what would that be?"

"I have a feeling I won't get good at conversation just by copying the masters. It's like my body won't be able to keep up…like I probably don't have the basic abilities to make the moves I want to make."

That's exactly the problem. I literally can't copy the experts. At least, that's how it often goes with video games—the expert is just too good with the controller.

I'm foreseeing the same problem in conversations. Say I want to introduce a new topic or respond to a joke with some witty comment, but the words just don't come out because I don't have the skills... In that sense, life really is a game.

"Very astute. You're right. You need to build up your skills."

"Right? And it won't happen overnight..."

"It's the easiest thing ever."

"Huh? It's easy?"

"Yep," Hinami said, raising her finger in the air like a cheerful teacher. "Just memorize."

"...Memorize?"

"Yeah. Piece of cake, right?"

She smiled mischievously. I was being teased.

"Come on, I need more than that. What do you mean?"

"It's very simple."

She pulled a pencil box from her bag. From inside it, she withdrew a pile of flash cards and started flipping through them.

"What are those?" I said, peering at the cards in her hand. I couldn't believe my eyes. "...You're kidding me!"

Each card had writing on both sides. For example, one said "The story about the little brother of Taro Nakajima (Group 2)" on the front and "He said he'd get into a national junior high no problem, but he didn't even take the entrance exam" on the back. Another one said "What my mom said to me in the middle of May" on the front with "You're a fine student but you wear the stupidest clothes" on the back. Another said "The scene in the third episode of *My Secret Father* that made me laugh" on the front and "The part where Yusuke Sugawara falls down, but he's being so careful not to get hurt that it looks like a slapstick routine" on the back. And on and on. There was a whole fat pile of them.

"See? Easy."

She was positively beaming. Terrifying.

"You...memorized these? Conversation topics?"

"Yup." The smile was affixed to her face like the mask of a leering ogre.

"No, this is just too weird..."

"What are you talking about? In RPGs, you memorize the attack and defense values for all the equipment, right? And in training-battle games, you memorize the fixed stats of all the monsters, right? What's the difference?"

As she was talking, she opened her large pencil box to show me the piles of flash cards stuffed inside, all of which I guessed served the same purpose as the ones she'd just shown me.

"Oh geez..."

"Why do you sound so pathetic? If you do this, you'll never run out of topics."

Sure, but...if a normal person saw this, they'd run the other way.

"...It's just, wow. You're right that I'm not gonna run out of topics..." *I can see her point, but...* "Are you suggesting I do the same thing?"

I was somewhat on the defensive.

"Obviously. But you can use whatever method you want. It doesn't have to be flash cards. You're decent at studying, right? In that case, you can use whatever is easiest for you as long as you memorize some topics."

"O-okay."

"Okay then, that's it as far as conversation instruction goes."

"Um, wait a second. There's something I don't understand."

"What?"

"Assuming I can memorize some topics, you know I always stutter when I talk to people. What should I do about that? Practice saying 'excuse me' or something?"

"...Just get used to it," Hinami said, sounding bored and tapping her finger on her forehead. "Anyway, you're not going to say 'excuse me' to kids in our class, so what's the point of practicing?"

"Oh r-right."

"I swear," she sighed, putting her flash cards back in the pencil box and sticking the box in her bag.

"Whew...I'm kinda tired after today," I said.

"Makes sense. We talked about a lot of new stuff. Plus you shared a lot of your own thoughts. But tonight when you get home, and then tomorrow night, I want you to review our conversation, because we went over a lot of important things."

"Review? You mean just try to remember what we talked about? I think I can do that...but I'm not sure."

"I thought as much. Here, take this."

She pulled a slender, palm-sized rectangular device with REPLAY and RECORD buttons on it from her chest pocket.

"...A recorder?"

"Yeah, it's a voice recorder. I've been taping our whole conversation."

When did she manage to do that?

"Ha-ha, you plan for everything... Did you buy that just for this?"

"No, I had it around. You can use it for a lot of things. I'm just lending it to you for a bit."

A lot of things... I wonder what that includes? Considering those flash cards, though, I'm too scared to ask. She handed the recorder to me.

"Th-thanks," I said.

"It has a bunch of different folders, but there's nothing in them. If you press the REPLAY button, you can listen to today's conversation. And here's the plug for earphones."

"G-got it."

She really thought of everything for me. Must be another skill of normie experts.

"Okay, so let's talk about the plan for tomorrow."

"Huh? Tomorrow? Isn't tomorrow Saturday?"

Some schools have class on Saturdays, but ours wasn't one of them.

"Yes, and that's why it's extra important. Or did you have plans?"

"No...I'm free." *Sadly enough.* "Why? You want me to practice at home or something?"

"Nope."

"What, then?"

She replied as if the answer was not a huge bombshell.

"We're meeting at Omiya Station at eleven AM. You're going to spend the day with me."

A date?! Or...I guess not, but...what?!

4

When a girl's your first friend, life feels like a date for a while

It was Saturday. I arrived in Omiya, whose claim to fame is being the biggest district in Japan people visit when they don't have the energy to go all the way to Tokyo for Ikebukuro or Shinjuku or whatever. Incidentally, if the prefecture finds out that you went to Ikebukuro when you just as well could have gone to Omiya, you'll be executed by Kobaton, Saitama's mascot.

"*Huff...puff...* Were you waiting long?"

"Nope, just got here," Hinami said with less intonation than a text-to-speech program. That was how I knew she was upset.

"I'm sorry!" I was one minute late.

"...I'm sure you were busy trying to find something to wear that wouldn't be too embarrassing, even though you don't actually own a single decent outfit. You're useless."

"...You know me so well."

When someone sees through you that completely, it's hard to even muster the energy to get depressed. That's how right she was.

"Well, I suppose your attitude has improved a little, considering what you wore the first time we got together."

"Oh, whatever."

Actually, it wasn't that. It was the enormity of being out and about in broad daylight next to Aoi Hinami. Did she even realize what a big deal that was? This was me trying to be considerate.

"Okay, let's get going."

"Wait a second. Tell me what today's goal is."

After all, she'd only told me to meet her, nothing else.

"Well... What do *you* think it is? Why would we come to Omiya for normie training?"

"Huh? A quiz?"

She wants me to think for myself, then? Okay. Hmm.

As I mulled over the question, I glanced at Hinami. She was still standing in front of our meeting spot, the Bean Tree sculpture in the station.

Seriously though, is it normal to look that good just standing there? She was wearing a long, lightweight blue coat (?) over a dress-like two-layer T-shirt (?). It was simple but oddly flattering. You could call the look cute, but you could also call it beautiful. I have no idea whether it was because of the quality of the materials or the style of the clothes. All I know is that looking at her felt like being face-to-face with a celebrity.

As I was thinking, staring absently at Hinami, I overheard two guys who looked like college students whispering to each other as they waited across the way from us.

"Is that...Hinami...?" one quietly asked, to which the other replied, "...Yeah, it's really her..." *Whoa. I was just comparing her to a celebrity, but what if she really is one...?* She was already overqualified for every other area of life; it wasn't impossible.

"...Hey, Hinami, you wouldn't happen to be a celebrity, would you?" I whispered to Hinami, who was now radiating disappointment.

"Where did that come from?"

"See those guys over there?" I began, then explained the situation.

"Oh... Well, I'm not a celebrity, but I *am* famous. Especially around here."

"Famous? How's that different from being a celebrity?"

"I'm not in showbiz, but I'm famous."

"What do you mean?"

"Well, I always have one of the top scores in the national practice exams, and last year I competed in a few cross-country running events at the national level... And then with my looks, my name gets around."

Top in the national practice exams? Competing in cross-country at the national level? Normal people would wait until just the right minute to reveal that stuff, then spend hours bragging about it. But she'd dropped it nonchalantly into the conversation in a single breath. I felt dizzy.

"Wait a second. I knew you were amazing, but not that amazing!"

At best, I figured she could beat anyone at our school. But nationally?

"I've been telling you this whole time. I'm confident I can win in any field."

She wasn't boasting—far from it, she treated all this like my questions were annoying.

"…How on earth do you get those kinds of results?"

"It's nothing special. I just think a little longer and work a little harder than everyone else in every field. Anyway, forget about that and tell me what you think your goal is for today."

She made it sound simple, but…

I might be walking around with a bigger fish than I realized.

"We came here so…I could get used to…crowds?"

"I think…your level might actually be much lower than I thought…"

She pressed her temples like she was totally fed up.

* * *

The first place she brought me was a bookstore. But why a bookstore?

"So what are we doing in here?"

"Studying… Or more like deciding on your direction."

"Direction?"

Hinami walked briskly toward the magazine corner and stopped in front of the fashion section.

"If you were teaching a beginner how to play *Atafami*, would you choose their character for them?"

By now, I was used to her suddenly talking about games.

"No. I mean, I'd stop them if they chose one that put them at a big disadvantage. Basically though, I'd want them to use a character they like and that's easy for them to use. I'd probably tell them which ones were easy."

Hinami nodded. "Right. Why?"

"Because they'd have more fun that way. If they're not having fun, they lose their motivation, and in the long run that would ruin the whole point."

"Exactly. That's why we came to the bookstore."

"...Huh?"

"Which of these styles do you like? I mean as a general inspiration."

She flipped through a magazine.

"It's hard to choose."

"Today, we're gonna buy some clothes for you based on whatever you choose. So what do you think?"

"...Oh, okay."

So I was choosing my character.

"Are you sure I should be making this decision? I don't have much fashion sense..."

"Don't worry. Everything in this magazine is gonna be stylish. Some of it wouldn't look good on you, but I'll stop you if you choose any of that."

"Got it."

All of it looked stylish to me. And all of it looked like too much for me. I probably wasn't tall enough or something. I spent about five minutes groaning as I examined the models until I finally chose one as a very general inspiration. *This one might be okay for me?*

"I don't know, I guess this one?"

I wasn't confident at all. Also, I noticed after I pointed that the price for the jacket was ¥44,800. *Uh, that's waaaay beyond my budget.*

"Okay, interesting choice...this should be fine," Hinami said, closing the magazine and pulling up a maps app up on her phone. "Let's go."

"Huh? Where?"

"It's obvious, isn't it? To a store where you can buy the clothes for that outfit."

I—I can't afford that!

The store we arrived at was the most fashionable place I'd ever seen. *So this is what clothing stores are like...* On the way, Hinami had pointed to an ATM and I'd taken out some money, somewhat under duress. The balance left me uneasy that buying one jacket would eat through my entire paltry savings.

"Um, Hinami? I'm broke. I can't be buying expensive clothes."

"Don't worry," she said, handing me a jacket.

"I mean, I really can't spend forty thousand... Huh?"

The number on the price tag read ¥9,720.

"Um...but you said we were going to the store that sold the clothes from that outfit."

"Yes, I did."

"Then why... Are the prices this different for the same store?"

"Nope. This store sells the shirt from that outfit."

"...Oh, I get it."

She hadn't said we were going to the store that sold the jacket brand. *What is this, some kind of trick question?*

"Fashion magazines usually include the brand names and prices of the clothes. When you find an outfit you like, check the prices. Look for the brand you can afford, and go to that store."

If all the clothes in that outfit were by expensive brands, she said I should look for another outfit until I found something that worked.

"If you do that, you can't really go wrong. The only item from this brand in the outfit you chose was the shirt, but any brand that makes it into a magazine, even if it's just one shirt, will make a fine outfit. So you should feel free to choose the rest of the outfit here."

Simple and clear.

"...Okay. I think I can handle that."

"I like that answer. Sounds like you're getting motivated to do things on your own."

"I told you, didn't I? I don't play around when it comes to games."

"Indeed you did." Hinami seemed happy.

"...And I still haven't learned the most important part."

"You mean how to choose the clothes?"

"Right. I don't know how to choose from so many options. What do I do?"

"That's the easiest part."

"The easiest? No way. Don't you need to help from all your taste and experience when you choose them? I can't imagine an easy attack strategy for that…"

"Of course. If you don't fully make use of taste and experience, you'll have a hard time picking out what's stylish. Fashion isn't something you can master overnight."

"…So…"

"Do you know what this is?"

Hinami cut me off and pointed up in front of us. There, dressed in a T-shirt, jacket, and pants was…

"A mannequin…"

"I bet you can guess what I'm going to say next." Her finger moved from the mannequin back toward me. "You're gonna buy that whole outfit."

Now that she said it, it did seem like an easy cheat. *She's right; I can't really mess up with this strategy.*

"Who do you think chose the clothes for this mannequin?"

"The people who work here?"

"Correct. And clothing store employees are usually more fashionable than your average person, right? You've gotta have a certain degree of confidence to get the job."

"I guess so. I'd never apply for a job like this."

"Mannequins are like advertisements inside the store to help sell clothes. These employees know their stuff, and they've put a lot of effort into thinking through their outfits."

"…Okay."

"What's more, several employees have probably talked it over together. That means multiple fashion-forward employees thought specifically about this one outfit. Foolproof, wouldn't you say?"

"Uh…yeah." I was convinced.

"You see? You said earlier that being fashionable is tough unless you have help from all your taste and experience."

"Yeah."

"In which case, you simply borrow the taste and experience of people with style. That's all there is to it."

"…Makes sense."

After all, the quickest route to improvement in *Atafami* was stealing, too. In this case, imitating the experts.

"Then you just wear that outfit as is. If you buy clothes that way a bunch of times, you'll start to get a sense for it, and you won't have to buy the whole mannequin anymore."

"Got it... Oh, can I ask a question?"

"What?"

"When you say 'buy the whole mannequin,' does the mannequin come with the clothes?"

"...Are you an idiot?"

Her reply was not a yes or a no, but an insult. From that, I deduced the answer was no.

After that, she told me to choose which of the three mannequin outfits I liked the most, which I did more or less on impulse.

"...Okay, now go try on the clothes." She made it sound so easy.

"What?! Try them on?!"

No-no-no, no way! Am I even allowed to try these things on? I mean, I'd have to talk to one of the fashionable people in their natural habitat. That's clearly impossible!

"Why are you so surprised? You're overly self-conscious. The store employee couldn't care less, so hurry up and do it."

"Wait a second! I thought I was safe if I bought the mannequin's outfit! Why do I need to try it on?!"

"The outfit should be fine, but the size might be wrong. With your build, you should be okay with a medium, but do it just to be sure. That way you'll know for next time."

"No...but, uh..."

The topic of size was uncharted territory for me, so I couldn't very well contradict her.

"Go on."

"Y-you want me to ask her?"

"Obviously. I'll want you to try things on when you go shopping by yourself in the future. You should practice asking on your own."

"Y-you want me to try things on in the future?"

"Yes, I do."

Her cold tone made it clear that further questions would be useless. I had no choice…

"…Wh-wh-what should I say…?" My voice was shaking. *What the hell?* Objectively, this was really sad.

"Just say, 'I'd like to buy the outfit on that mannequin. Can I try it on?' Or something like that."

"Huh? Um, so 'I'd like to buy the outfit on that mannequin.'"

"'Can I try it on?'"

"'I'd like to buy the outfit on that mannequin. Can I try it on?' Like that?"

"Yep."

I was asking for so much help I might as well have been in recovery after a major injury. Or in a nursing home. *Sorry, Hinami…*

"'…I'd like to buy the outfit on that mannequin. Can I try it on?' Okay, I've got this!"

I steeled my will and walked up to the store employee. It was a t-teenage girl. And her hair was in a ponytail, revealing the beautiful nape of her neck. *Yikes.*

"Um, 'scuse me!"

Okay, so far, so good!

"How can I help you?"

"Um, that, that—" I stuttered, pointing to the mannequin.

"You mean that one?"

"Yes. Um…I'd like to buy that mannequin."

You see? I just asked to buy the mannequin. This is horrible. Nevertheless…

"…Um, you'd like the outfit the mannequin is wearing? Would you like to try it on?"

"Yes, please!"

Thanks to this incredibly understanding employee, this was working out well, if not quite according to plan.

After navigating these various twists and turns, I tried on the clothes, received Hinami's stamp of approval, and obtained a coordinated, fashionable outfit for about thirty thousand yen.

*   *   *

"Ooh, why don't you put it on right now?"

After I paid for the clothes, I heard a very cheerful voice right next to my ear. *Who is that? Oh right. That's Hinami's fake voice.*

"Would you like to wear the outfit out of the store?" the employee asked.

"Yes, do it!"

Her peerless, perfect smile was aimed in my direction. It could only mean one thing: *Put it on,* now.

"…Uh, yes, please."

The employee led me over to the changing room, and I put on the outfit. She folded up the clothes I'd been wearing and put them in the bag.

"It looks great on you," she commented when I came out of the room. I blushed a little.

As I was marveling over the great customer service here, the employee whispered something into my ear in passing, too quiet for Hinami to hear.

"Your girlfriend is so adorable and nice! You should take good care of her!" She smiled at me impishly.

"Oh, she's not my girlfriend!" I said, flustered.

"Oh right. Of course not," she replied.

Hey! Why 'of course' not? Okay, it's true, but still!

"All right, we have a little time before the hair appointment."

"…You already made an appointment, huh."

Hinami's preference for extremely thorough planning wasn't much of a surprise by this point.

"How about we kill some time by…getting a bite to eat?" she suggested.

This should have been the part where my heart started pounding out of control, but somehow it wasn't exactly like that.

"Oh, great idea. I was just getting hungry. Should we find a diner or something? Or since we're in Omiya, how about an Omiya specialty? Wait, I forgot, there are no Omiya specialties. Too bad there aren't any *sakitama* rice balls around here. Ha-ha."

For some reason, Hinami responded to my joke with a glare verging on contempt. Incidentally, a *sakitama* rice ball is a Saitama classic: a little bread bun made from rice. Just as rice is the staple of Japan and taro root is the staple of some Southeast Asian countries, the *sakitama* rice ball is the beloved staple of Saitama.

"Listen. You're about to go out to eat with a girl, and not just any girl—Aoi Hinami. Do you really think it's a good idea to go to some random chain restaurant with no atmosphere whatsoever?"

"No, but things aren't like that between us."

"Never mind that. There's a hamburger place near here."

"Really? Have you been there?"

"Not yet."

"Huh. And? Are you planning some kind of special hamburger restaurant training there?"

"Not particularly."

"No? Really? So why go to a burger place?"

"Because I want to eat there."

"That's it?"

"…Yes."

"You just want to eat a hamburger? Aoi Hinami just wants a hamburger?"

"…What? Is there something wrong with that?"

"No, but…" I was figuring she must have chosen that restaurant with some sort of practice in mind. "So you like hamburgers, huh?"

"Shut up! How many times are you going to say that? …My friends just like that place. Let's get going."

She started walking. *Huh. She just wanted to eat there. That's oddly normal of her. Very unexpected.*

The hamburger restaurant she brought me to was a cute little place; an ad might tout it as a "forest hideaway." There was a round wooden table out front, sheltered by a parasol and accompanied by a pair of stools that looked like tree stumps next to it. The whole thing was straight out of a picture book.

We walked inside and sat down at a table for two. I glanced over the menu and picked something in about two seconds, then waited for Hinami to decide on her order. Three minutes or so passed, and she was still silently and intently scrutinizing the menu.

"…Wonder what I should order."

"You're really having trouble deciding, huh?"

"You look like you made up your mind already… What are you getting?"

She sounded uncharacteristically hesitant. Which was surprising because I would have expected her to say, *I couldn't care less what you order. I'm getting what I want.*

"The cheeseburger with tomato."

"Hmm, that does sound good. It really does…"

She brought the tip of her finger to her lips and nodded with the gravity of a detective trying to solve a crime.

"H-Hinami…?"

"Fumiya Tomozaki-kun, I'd like to make a suggestion."

"Huh?" Why was she calling me by my full name? She looked deadly serious.

"I'm going to get the Japanese-style hamburger stuffed with cheese and sauce. So…"

"Yeah?"

"What would you think about splitting that and your burger?" she said, now with the gravity of a detective announcing that the missing murder weapon had just been found. I couldn't help it; I burst out laughing.

"…What are you laughing at? Are you trying to upset me?"

"Oh sorry," I said, still smiling a little.

"I want the tomato cheeseburger, and I also want the stuffed burger. All I did was make a rational proposal to resolve the issue. There's nothing to laugh about."

"R-right, of course. Sure, let's split it. You like cheese, huh?" I replied, remembering that she'd ordered the carbonara at the pasta place last time.

"Shut up! I can like whatever I want! So we've decided, we're splitting those two things? …And how long are you gonna keep smiling? It really is irritating. Hurry up and order."

It really would have been rude to keep smiling at this point, so with a little effort, I managed to suppress my grin and order. We sipped at the water the waiter had brought while we waited for our hamburgers to come.

"By the way, did you listen to the voice recording?"

She was talking about the recorder she'd handed me at yesterday's review meeting. I'd followed her instructions and listened to it before going to bed.

"Yeah, I did."

"How was it? Did you notice anything?"

"Like what?"

I was relistening to the same stuff I'd heard the previous day after school, most of which I already remembered, so there wasn't much to notice…

"Maybe I should rephrase. Did you notice anything aside from the content?"

"Aside from the content…? …Oh."

"I see you did."

"…Our voices."

I *had* noticed. The content was basically what I remembered, but one thing was different from how I remembered the conversation.

"My voice—or maybe like, the way I talked? It was totally different…"

"Right?" she said, like she'd been waiting for me to say that.

"Yeah. People always say your voice sounds different from how you imagine it, but I'd never listened to such a long everyday conversation like that before… It was pretty surprising. I kinda drone, don't I?"

"…Yeah. If you noticed it the first time you listened, you'll be able to fix it."

"Think so?"

"Definitely. That's what they say to tone-deaf people—once you can tell your own voice is weird, you'll be able to fix it with practice. To a certain degree."

"Huh."

I felt like I'd heard that before—that the only people who were truly tone deaf were the ones who couldn't tell something was off.

"…But you're a particularly bad droner. You'd benefit from some training to correct it."

"Am I really that bad?"

"Yes. It's because you depend too heavily on the words themselves."

"I depend too heavily on words?"

"For example, when I explain something, you have a number of set responses, like 'Makes sense' and 'Really?'"

"I do?"

"Yeah. It's probably unconscious. Well, you're probably aware that always saying the same thing would be rude...so you change the words, but the tone's the same."

"The tone's the same?"

"Yes. You don't use facial expressions or inflection or gestures much in conversations. Your tone is always flat."

"Oh." She could be right.

"I'm going to give you an assignment while we're having lunch."

"An assignment?"

"Yes. What I want you to do is..."

"Yes?"

"From now on, when you respond to something I say, you're only allowed to use vowels."

"Only vowels?" *What does that have to do with tone?*

"You don't understand, do you? Listen. Only using vowels means you can only say things like *Oh? Ah! Oo!*"

"Okay... Oh, we haven't started yet, have we?"

"Not yet. Anyway, you know what happens when your options are limited like that? How do you think you'll communicate your thoughts to me?"

"...Oh, I get it."

"You'll have to express yourself through your facial expressions, tone, volume, and gestures, right?"

"...Yeah."

"In other words..."

Hinami drew her eyebrows together and said "Oh?" in a threatening voice, then made her eyes round and said "Oh!" as if she'd just discovered something. Next, she made a kind of dumb expression and gave an "Oh..." of realization. Finally, she held her head in both hands and groaned "Ohhh!" with frustration.

"…As you've just seen, you can express a lot with just 'Oh.' Once you're in the habit of communicating your feelings through inflection, gestures, facial expression, and volume, the droning issue will clear up on its own."

"…You're sure good at that."

The first thing I'd noticed was her incredible acting ability. That and how gracefully she modeled her examples. It was really cute.

"This is a way for you to narrow down the words you use and focus on other ways of expressing yourself so you can naturally improve. To put it another way, you've been using a wide variety of words, so your ability to express yourself in other ways has atrophied."

"…Okay, I basically get it."

"Good. Then we'll start now. You don't need to follow the rule when you're saying something of your own, just when you're reacting."

I figured I'd start with a vowel that was right for starting something new…

"Oh!" I said energetically, holding up a determined fist next to my face.

"I like the enthusiasm, especially when we've only just started. You might be a natural at this."

She's praising me…in which case…

"Eyyy!" I cheered, throwing my arms up. That was all I could come up with after considering a bunch of options.

"Great! Making a fool of yourself. I thought you'd be too embarrassed at first to do more than tiny gestures."

She had just insulted me. So if I wanted to say *"Stop messing with me"*…

"Eh?" I growled, pulling my eyebrows together discontentedly.

"You're like a fish out of water. You seem a little angry. But what do you think? It's good training, right? How about you pay for lunch to thank me?"

To express *Hey, wait just a second now!*…

"Ah!" I yelped, thrusting my hands out jokingly. Just then…

"Sorry for the wait. One Japanese-style stuffed burger…Huh? Tomozaki…kun?"

Out of the blue, the waitress said my name.

"Oh!" I replied, still riding the wave of the vowel training. I looked up at the girl who had brought the hamburger to find someone who was halfway between a character from a picture book and a girl's manga—my classmate Fuka Kikuchi-san. The one from the nose-blowing incident. She was wearing glasses, which she usually didn't. They looked amazing on her.

"Ah?!" I cried. Maybe I'd gotten the hang of the vowel thing a little too well.

"Fuka-chan?! Wow, I didn't know you worked here! What a coincidence!"

Just as I was wondering how a third classmate had shown up, I realized it was Hinami, the social quick-change artist.

"Yes, I do… I just started about a week ago because I'd heard good things about it…"

"Everyone's been talking about this place at school lately! I wanted to try it out, so we stopped by today for the first time."

"Yeah, exactly!" I said, but I was still making the exaggerated gestures.

"Oh…yes… But, why…?"

"Why what?" Hinami said. I think she probably knew what Kikuchi-san was trying to say, but she didn't let it show. Kikuchi-san's gaze shifted back and forth between us curiously, as if she was seeing a pair of fairies that no one else could.

"…So you two are friends… That's a surprise…"

"I know! We just got to know each other recently, in home ec," Hinami answered right away. She sure was good at lying.

"…Oh, that time."

Kikuchi-san giggled. Her long eyelashes quivered bewitchingly behind her glasses.

"Oh sorry! That one's mine," Hinami said, pointing to the plate Kikuchi-san was still holding.

"Oh right. Here you go… Well, enjoy yourselves…" With that graceful smile, she fit into the forestlike ambiance of the restaurant perfectly.

"…Is she gone?"

"Yeah."

"Um…you think she figured it out? I mean, everything?"

For a second, Hinami was silent. "I think we're okay. Even if she heard my voice for a second, she probably thought I was imitating someone. I wouldn't have let her overhear a long conversation. Since this place is so popular with kids at school, I suspected we might run into someone we knew."

"Oh, okay."

That hadn't even occurred to me. Typical for someone with a communication block.

"But I was surprised she was working here. I wasn't ready for that, so my reaction was a little slow. She had those glasses on, too... But I know now, so it's fine. I won't slip up."

...I knew her well enough to know that was true.

"It'll be hard to continue now. If it had been an ordinary classmate, we could have gone on practicing responses, but...Fuka Kikuchi is different."

"...What do you mean? If it had been an ordinary classmate?"

Was there something special about Kikuchi-san?

"During the exercises last week, I saw the possibility—and based on the reactions I just saw, I'm sure of it."

"Sure of what?"

Hinami grinned.

"Fuka Kikuchi is going to be your first love interest."

* * *

It goes without saying that I couldn't look Kikuchi-san in the eyes when she came back a few minutes later with my tomato cheeseburger, but I was a mess even before that.

"W-w-wait a second! Just wh-what do you mean by that?"

"Judging by how flustered you are, I think you already know," Hinami said casually, tilting her mug.

"Y-y-you mean, d-d-dating Kikuchi-san...?"

My emotions were spinning out of control, but obviously I couldn't speak loudly, so my answer came out sounding pretty weird.

"Exactly. Your mid-range goal is to get a girlfriend before the end of the school year. She's going to be the one."

Hinami seemed to be keeping her voice deliberately calm. She was teasing me for being so worked up. But I had no idea what to ask or say, so for the moment I just sputtered "Wh-wh-why?"

"There are various reasons."

Hinami took a bite of her hamburger, chewed, then swallowed. She was clearly going out of her way to keep me in suspense.

"The main reason is that of the four girls you talked to, you have the best chance with her."

"Chance?"

I have a chance? With Kikuchi-san?

"Half."

"Huh?" I was confused by the abrupt comment.

"Your burger?"

"Oh right."

She sure was drawing out this conversation. *Tease. Or maybe she just really wants a bite of my burger.* For the moment, I focused on splitting the burgers.

"I don't know why, but I got a glimpse of it when you talked to Yuzu," she said, pointing to my nose. "When Yuzu asked Fuka-chan for a tissue, her response was really quick, right?"

"Well, now that you mention it...yeah... But, why?"

"As soon as you asked Yuzu for the tissue, Fuka-chan started searching for hers, even though she was only listening in on the conversation."

"Wow..." *I didn't even notice.* "...Is that all?" I asked.

"No. That was just a glimpse. Afterward, it struck me as a little unnatural, but it could have just been that she's nice to everyone—not necessarily that she likes you. But it could also mean she didn't especially *dislike* you."

"Yeah. And?"

"It's like this," Hinami said, pointing to her stuffed burger. "When she brought my food, she realized who we were, right? Do you remember what she said?"

"Uh...? Did she say something important?"

"Yes. She said, 'Huh? Tomozaki-kun?'"

She pointed at me like she'd just dropped a bombshell.

"...So what? It's normal to call your classmate by their name."

She sighed, then put her hand on her chest. "Even if they're with the famous Aoi Hinami?"

"Oh. I see."

That was a convincing point. Convincing, but also a reminder of her impressive self-confidence.

"I'm a fairly big star at our high school. And I'm approachable, too. Normally, when someone bumps into a group I'm a part of, they always say my name first. But the first thing Fuka-chan said was 'Tomozaki-kun?' It may seem unimportant, but it was actually the clincher."

She was dead serious. Knowing how confident she was about everything, it scared me.

"Was it really such a big deal?"

"Yes, it was. Think about it. Even if it didn't involve a big star like me, if you're a girl and you see a guy and a girl you know, it's easier to talk to the girl first, right? So if she says the guy's name first..."

"That does...make sense."

"It may seem normal to you that she said your name, but it was actually out of the ordinary. Of course, if she hadn't noticed I was here, that would be a different story, but I have such a strong presence it's basically impossible not to notice me. So this either means you have a chance, or Fuka-chan just notices things differently from most people," Hinami said, polishing off her burger.

"Are you sure we can rule out the possibility she didn't notice you?"

Hinami ignored my question and continued. "But as far as I know, she's a normal girl...which means there's probably some hope for you... Have you noticed anything?"

"Noticed anything?" I said, racking my brain. "Nope, nothing."

"Hmm," Hinami replied, looking troubled. "Maybe I'm misinterpreting it..."

For once, she seemed to have lost confidence in herself.

"If you're misinterpreting it, don't you think we should forget the whole love interest thing?"

"Not at all," she said firmly. "In either case, she's the best match for you right now. Even if I'm mistaken, she's still going to be your main love interest."

"B-but I'm not even sure if I like her or not." I was never really on board with this, and that was why.

"...Don't you think she's cute?" Hinami suddenly asked sharply.

"Huh?"

"Fuka-chan, I mean. I think she's very cute, but what do you think?"

"Um...well...I do, but..."

"Right. That's enough, isn't it? You don't know if you like her yet, but you're a little bit interested because she's cute. So you try approaching her, and that's how you know how you really feel... What's wrong with that?"

"Well, if you put it like that..."

"You won't be worrying about every little detail for several more levels."

Every little detail? Were my feelings really so insignificant? I was torn. My distaste for insincerity was getting mixed up with my fear of approaching her and my ego as a gamer. But...

"...I made up my mind to give this game all I've got. I'll do it," I declared. The initial decision was already made, so I might as well put aside my doubts and give it a try. *I can think about it later. It's too early to softlock myself here...right?*

"Nice. I knew you'd say yes," Hinami said, picking up the menu.

"You're getting dessert?"

"Yeah. You want anything? I heard the cake here is great."

"Really?" I said, scanning the menu. "Then I'll get the tiramisu."

"I'll have the chee—" Hinami broke off mid-word, blushing.

"Chee?"

She was suddenly extremely calm. Unnaturally calm. Fake.

"I'll have the cheesecake," she said in a tone that was as unnaturally calm as her expression.

When I burst out laughing again, she kicked me under the table.

After lunch we headed to the salon, where everything went smoothly and uneventfully. Hinami instructed me to ask for a safe haircut and otherwise leave it up to the barber, which I did. She also told me to get my eyebrows trimmed, and I did that too. After what the employee had said to me at the clothing store, I was ready to dive in headfirst. The total came to ¥4,800, which is ¥3,800 more than I usually spend.

When I looked in the mirror, I saw my ugly face topped off by a more-stylish-than-usual hairstyle. *Welp, I did it. And now I'm sad.*

That finished off a Saturday of learning how to pick out clothes, request a haircut and eyebrow trim, and improve my tone when speaking. Around evening, Hinami finally released me.

When I got home, I felt like I had finally advanced a little in the game for the first time.

"I'm back!"

I kicked off my shoes, more exhausted than usual, and stumbled into the living room. My parents weren't there, but my sister was sprawled on the sofa like an idiot wearing basically nothing on her legs except…I think they're called "short-shorts"?

"…You're such a slob," I said, not beating around the bush. She didn't look up.

"What? Like you have *any* room to talk! I mean, you're—" she said, finally glancing over at me. "…Huh?"

Her eyes were bulging in obvious bewilderment, like she was witnessing something beyond her wildest imaginings. She ran her eyes over me from head to toe.

"…Fumiya…um…"

* * *

"Hinami! Hinami!"

It was the following Monday morning. I sprinted up to Hinami, who had arrived in Sewing Room #2 before me.

"…Would you stop, please? You're acting like a dog with attachment issues."

"Your metaphor's bad enough without the last part!"

"Well, you sure are full of comebacks this morning."

"I may have cleared my first small goal!" I announced proudly.

Hinami's eyes flashed. "Really?! Was it someone in your family? They said something?"

Her eyes were definitely sparkling. Somehow, seeing that made me happy, too.

"Yeah, my sister! Listen to this and tell me if it counts!"

"Okay, but are you sure you didn't misinterpret something?"

"Mostly!"

"So what did she say?"

"Well…"

I could have used a drumroll right about then.

"She said, '…Fumiya…um…I don't think you could have pulled off that transformation without some help… What, did you read a book on how to de-geek yourself and get some sex appeal or something?'"

Hinami's expression was a strange mixture of bemused and chagrined satisfaction.

"Yeah, you cleared the goal, but…you sure seem happy about what your sister said."

"Shut up! A win's a win!"

"Okay, fine. Congratulations on achieving your first goal. Nice work."

"Th-thanks," I said, flustered.

"You might be thinking that you didn't do any of this yourself, but that's not true. Sure, you bought an outfit off a mannequin and got someone to cut your hair, but you're the one who decided to do it and had the will to come along with me. You're the one who worked every day to improve your expression and your posture. That's no small feat, and it led you to this outcome. It wasn't your effort alone, but *you're* the one who grabbed it with your own two hands. No question."

Hinami looked me straight in the eye as she spoke, fluently put into words what had been niggling at me.

"So I'll say it again: Congratulations."

"…Wow. Thank you."

Since she'd said all that, the second time around I was able to say "thank you" with a little more sincerity. I'd reached one goal in the game of life.

"Okay, then," Hinami said, briskly launching into her next topic without giving me a chance to bask in the afterglow of my success. "I'm going to announce your next small goal."

"You don't waste much time."

"Of course not. We need to make steady progress if you're going to achieve results. There's no way around it but step by step."

"I know, I know."

"Then I'll announce the goal. It's very simple."

I didn't even have time to gulp.

"Your goal is to go somewhere with a girl from school other than me. Just the two of you."

"Wait a second now!"

I reflexively pushed out my hands to stop her.

"…What? Are you planning to make some irrelevant complaint that reveals just how uncool and unready you are to join the real world?"

"No, but admit it! That goal is weird!"

"Why?"

"Because if I'm out alone with a girl, it's practically a date!"

For some reason, Hinami met my fervent and logical argument with a look that went beyond heartfelt exasperation to something bordering on affection.

"Huh? I'm assuming you've never dated anyone, but haven't you ever watched a rom-com on TV or read a comic about a relationship?"

"Yeah, a couple of times."

"So you should know this. In this day and age, not even a kid in junior high would assume two people were dating just because they went somewhere together."

"…R-really?" I was losing confidence.

"Really. Of course, it's true that a lot of times when people go out, they're testing the waters to see if they like each other enough to date."

"S-see…!" I said, clinging to the web the spider had dangled in front of me.

"Were you going to say something else?"

I was shrinking second by second beneath her withering gaze.

"Uh, um…well, I guess…that's that?"

"Yes. In any case, I'd like you to push ahead toward that goal. Are you ready? Here's what I want you to do today."

She continued without skipping a beat.

"Talk to Yuzu Izumi at least twice."

"Wait a second!" This time I had her for sure.

"Can you stop interrupting me?"

"It's not that! This one really is weird! The other day, you said Fuka Kikuchi was supposed to be my love interest, right? Shouldn't I be talking to her instead of Yuzu Izumi?" I argued forcefully, before realizing that was silly. "…I mean, I'm sure you just said the wrong name."

It was embarrassing, acting like I'd slain a dragon when Hinami's tongue had just slipped. Okay, maybe I did want to get her back a little for always cutting me down… But just as these thoughts were passing through my mind, she caught me off guard with her response.

"What are you talking about! I want you to talk to Yuzu Izumi, not Fuka Kikuchi!"

"Huh? …No need to be stubborn—you misspoke, didn't you?"

"…Listen. This is Aoi Hinami you're talking to. Do you think I 'misspeak'?"

"You mean to say you don't do that, either?"

"Just listen. Fuka Kikuchi is your love interest, but romance works differently in the game of life than it does in your typical dating sim."

"…What do you mean?"

"Here's the deal," she replied. "In dating sims, once you decide on your love interest, all you have to do is charge ahead, choose the options that make her like you more, and you've got her."

"Yeah…"

"But it doesn't work like that in real life. There's no set path."

"That makes sense, but why does that mean I should talk to Yuzu Izumi?"

"Okay, let's say you're playing a shooter."

Here we go.

"When can you maneuver more smoothly? When you don't have lives left, or when you do?"

"Huh?" I replied, confused for a second. "Well, it depends on your personality, but…I think the majority of people get nervous and don't play as well once they run out of lives. That's what happens to me."

"Hexactly."

"There it is!"

"Typically, you move better if you have room to fail."

"…So what's your point?"

She sighed, as she often did. "The same is true with romance."

"Meaning…?"

"You still don't get it? If there's only one girl you have a chance with and not a single other candidate if things fall through, it's like not having any lives left."

"Oh right."

"Continuing the analogy, if you have several candidates you could date if things don't work out, you're going to be more relaxed and confident about the whole thing, right?"

"Oh, that's what you mean." *I understand, but…* "You're talking about having a backup, right? But, Hinami—Yuzu Izumi? Really? That's not possible. It's me you're talking about here," I told her with unusual confidence.

"I'm not talking specifically about Yuzu Izumi. I'm just saying you can maintain a better mental and emotional state that way."

"Okay, but even so…wouldn't that be insincere?"

Having multiple backups sure seemed dishonest to me.

"You wouldn't be lying to anyone. It's just that if you make a couple of female friendships that could develop into romantic relationships, it helps you worry less."

"But I wouldn't be giving my whole heart to her."

"Oh, come on, this is getting silly. The reason Japan's international policy can't keep up with the rest of the world is because everyone here has blind faith in empty words. 'Sincerity' and 'giving your whole heart' just sound good on the surface; they actually distract everyone from taking productive steps."

Whoa, why're we talking about international affairs all of a sudden?

I thought for a second. "But wouldn't it be self-defeating if Kikuchi-san ended up liking me less as a result?" I asked.

"That won't happen. Granted, in typical dating sims, when you make choices that increase another character's affection for you, the affection of your main love interest goes down."

"Right?"

"But real life is different. Here, when one girl's affection goes up, so does the other girl's."

Uh, so... "...You mean my reputation would improve among girls in general?"

"Yeah, that's a simple way to put it. It can also make girls want you all for themselves, improve your status as a male, and have many other effects."

"Huh, really...? Okay, I understand." I highly doubted that my reputation among girls would improve, but anyway. "...So I'm not going to do anything special for Kikuchi-san? She is my main love interest, after all."

"No, nothing special," Hinami said, then stopped. *Well, she must have some plan.*

"...Okay. But I'm not going to go so far that I'm being insincere."

"That's your prerogative. Just make sure you're not doing logical backflips to get away from this."

To tell the truth, I wasn't really worried about it, because you have to be pretty smooth to be accused of being a player, and I couldn't imagine that yet.

"Got it. All things considered, that approach should work... Plus, if I don't do it, it will take a long time to reach my mid-range goal."

After all, getting a girlfriend before I moved up a grade was completely insane to start with.

"That's true," Hinami said, nodding. "It's very important to keep your goals in sight."

"Okay…I'll give it a try."

"Also, there's the question of what to talk to her about."

"Oh, I did memorize some topics…"

Hinami reacted with some surprise, then smiled happily. "In that case, I'll leave it up to you," she said.

Talking to Yuzu Izumi twice… The old me would have given up completely as soon as I heard that idea. But now a small seed of self-confidence was sprouting, telling me I might be able to do it if I tried. It was a strange feeling.

"Oh, by the way—that's your assignment for every day this week."

"What?!"

That tender sprout was nipped in the bud.

5

Powerful techniques and equipment make it fun and easy to progress

On the Saturday I went out with Hinami and the following Sunday, I had diligently memorized conversation topics and practiced reacting with actual intonation like she'd taught me, in addition to continuing my expression and posture training.

To memorize the topics, I used one of my standard study techniques, which is to write with a red pen and then use a red translucent sheet to block out the answers. I'd managed to come up with ten, and I committed them all to memory. Response practice was a little harder, since there's no one I really talk to, and my mom and dad…well, we don't talk much, either. I had to resort to turning on the TV and reacting alongside the guests on talk shows. It was pretty sad.

While I was doing that, I noticed something. I thought my reactions were exaggerated because I could use only vowels, but there wasn't much difference between my tone and that of the guests on the shows. And yet when I watched TV as a passive spectator, their responses didn't seem overdone. Meaning what I considered too much would probably seem natural to people around me. Man, I must have come across really gloomy before.

"Whoo boy, I sure got a lot to learn!!" I declared as cheerfully as I could, sticking my chest out and holding my mouth in a semblance of a smile. I felt so unlike myself I couldn't help laughing.

I was sure I'd be able to achieve all sorts of things the old me hadn't been able to.

Monday in class:

"Hey, Izumi-san, did you do the English translation?"

The question may have sounded off-the-cuff and confident—and I hope more than anything that it did—but in reality, my heart was pounding. The whole way from Sewing Room #2 to the classroom I'd been psyching myself up and repeating, "Gonna say it, gonna say it, gonna say it," so when I sat down in class I was able to say it without a weird long pause first. Of course, the English translation was one of the topics I'd memorized in advance.

"Huh? Tomozaki-kun? What, did you not?"

The response revealed her surprise, but since I'd started a conversation, she didn't have much choice aside from answering.

"No, I did."

Izumi-san looked at me blankly. No, today was going to be different!

"So…what?"

She had shrunk back in her seat a little, staring at me. Her guard was going up. *Uh-oh, am I in trouble? No, everything's still fine. That's just one life down; I have more topics!*

"Didn't you think the weird English names were funny? Like, where did 'Marcus Purdy' come from?" I said, calling upon the most natural tone and expression I could muster.

"Marcus…? Sorry, I don't know what you're talking about. I mean, I haven't even started the translation yet…"

…Um. What do I do now? What were the other topics I memorized? Wait a second. What? Um. I should still have more than ten left. Huh? My mind was a complete blank.

The vast assurance of a moment earlier had been swept away without a trace, leaving only my strangely distant heartbeat.

"Oh really?" I chirped desperately. I was so upset I have no idea how it came out.

"Yeah. But why'd you bring it up all of a sudden? Was that it?"

"Uh, yeah, sorry," I said, suspecting that this time I'd completely failed to maintain the cheerful tone.

"It's fine, but…are you done?"

"Um, well…"

"What?"

"Um…oh, never mind."

After I gave her a wimpy excuse for a "yes," Izumi-san tilted her head quizzically, then headed over to the spot by the back windows where the normies always hung out.

I'd thought I might be able to pull this off after all my efforts, but it was a total failure. *Ha-ha-ha. What the heck? No, you should have expected this. This is you we're talking about. What were you thinking? Don't forget who you are. This is how you've always been. No way can you pull this off.*

I wasn't ready for field trials yet, Hinami.

With my fighting spirit and confidence totally wiped out, I didn't hear a word the teacher said. All I could think about was what Hinami would say to me during the review session after school, and how I would defend myself. But during the break between second and third period, when I got back from the bathroom, there was a note written on the worksheet I'd left out on my desk, letting me know she didn't give a damn.

"Twice every day," it read.

Are you serious…? Hinami, come on. You're telling me to go through that hell one more time…?

"Whew—!"

My broken confidence had led me astray momentarily, but *Atafami* and other games had instilled in me a hatred of losing. I spurred that side of myself into action, manually reigniting my fighting spirit. If I gave up now, I'd be losing to myself. *Smack!* I slapped both my cheeks. *You decided to do this, so do it. You decided to do this, so do it. The time to drop the game is when you decide the whole thing is garbage, and not before. Keep going until then.*

Anyway, Izumi-san wasn't my main love interest, and we hadn't interacted much to start with. *Doesn't matter! Everything's fine! Even if things did get weird, it was just one embarrassing hiccup! No worries!*

I gave myself a little pep talk as I waited for the right moment to talk to her again, but somehow I failed after third period, and again during lunch, and again after fifth period.

It would have been one thing if there were no opportunities, but running scared from perfectly good chances was nonsense. *Argh, this isn't gonna work!* Somehow, I had to find the willpower to make this happen.

It was after school, right after the teacher finished the last class. If I let this chance go, Yuzu Izumi would probably go over to the back windows again to meet up with the other normies and go home from there. This was really and truly my final chance. I still had a stock of memorized conversation topics on hand. It wouldn't be too weird. *You're fine!*

I took a deep breath and squeezed out a couple of words.

"Um, Izumi-san?"

My voice was so quiet only I could hear it.

Naturally, she didn't notice I'd spoken to her. As always, she joined her usual group and headed home.

"I commend you for even showing up here."

Hinami and I were in Sewing Room #2 after school. It was like she could see straight into my soul.

"…I'm sorry."

The apology came out naturally. I really did feel awful. Depressed, even, and that's no exaggeration.

"If I were your friend, I'd probably try to comfort you," Hinami said. My head was lowered, so she couldn't see my face. "But I'm your instructor. If I am your friend, I'm a war buddy. So I'll stick to instructing you." Every word she said was true. "Today's review meeting will be short. I have two things to say."

"Just two?"

"Yes. First, if you look to me for comfort, it's over. If you make excuses, it's over. I want you to think long and hard about what went wrong."

Her eyes flashed severely.

"…Y-yes, ma'am!"

Her words echoed forcefully in my mind.

"Second, I want you to keep it up with the same attitude tomorrow."

"…Huh?"

"What you did today was nothing I didn't foresee. I knew there was a chance this would happen when I gave you the assignment. It's not a problem; you're still learning. But you're to make every effort to meet the quota of two times per day. That's all. Understand?"

"Nothing you didn't foresee?"

"Yes. So you absolutely must continue tomorrow."

"But…honestly speaking, I don't know if I have the confidence to talk to her again…and my topic was dead in the water."

"Today was a coincidence. Yuzu happened to have not done the translation, so the conversation was over before it began. But the topic itself wasn't that bad, and your tone and expression were passable. Barely."

"R-really?"

"Yes."

"But I don't know if my other topics are any good…"

"You're worrying too much. You can start a conversation about pretty much anything. If you're out of ideas, the other person can be the topic, like their expression or hairstyle. Seriously, anything is fine."

"R-really…?"

"Yes. If you continue with the same attitude tomorrow, it's highly likely that a normal conversation will take place."

"…But…"

"Oh, come on, stop it with the *but*s! Listen to me. *But* isn't a word for making excuses and running away from your problems. It's a word you use to get compromises and move in a better direction. Did I say anything that wasn't true? Just shut up and do it."

Then out of nowhere, she grabbed my butt.

"Aieee?!"

"You're working on your posture even while I'm lecturing you, and that's the best proof of all that you're making a genuine effort. Okay? I'm not saying that all effort pays off, but this kind, the kind aimed at a reasonable goal, will pay off for anyone as long as they do it right."

"Hinami…"

You're actually…

"…What? No, don't say anything. You're probably worrying about something irrelevant again, right? If you have time for that, then spend it thinking back on what you've done so far and thinking ahead to what you should do from here on out. You've got more problems than you know. You're a poisoned, confused blockhead wearing cursed equipment."

I'd been on the verge of thinking she was actually a kind person. Very dangerous.

The next day arrived. If Hinami said so, then maybe I really did have a good chance of getting a conversation going, just by doing the same thing as before. I mean, it basically made sense. Starting a conversation shouldn't in itself be so hard. Even I could manage conversations with my family, and with Hinami. And I'd gotten by with Mimimi, too. I should be okay as long as I had a topic and decent presentation. Beyond that, all I needed was courage…right?

After returning home yesterday in a funk, I got an e-mail from Hinami with some information about Yuzu Izumi's friends and stuff. I used that to prepare another ten topics, which I memorized perfectly. I was extra thorough so I'd be able to remember them even if I got nervous and panicked. I was in good shape…at least, that was the impression I was hoping to create.

I didn't have any chances to talk to her in homeroom, but after first period ended, an opportunity rolled around.

Here goes nothing!
"Hey, Izumi-san."

Yuzu Izumi looked back at me. Very dramatically—well, dramatically for me, anyway—I lowered my voice and continued.

"Um, do you think Nakamura is still mad at me?"

"What?"

She seemed briefly confused, but then she lowered her voice like me and smiled a little.

"Ha-ha-ha, why are you asking *me*?"

Her natural, happy smile melted some of my nervousness, and I answered without any awkward pauses.

"Well…I heard you two are good friends."

"What? Who said that?"

"Um…"

Might as well be honest. "Hinami."

We were whispering back and forth. I couldn't do much with tone at this volume, so I concentrated on my facial expressions.

"Oh. You and Aoi sure are friendly these days, aren't you, Tomozaki-kun? Is something going on?!"

"No way, nothing's going on!"

"Really…?" she asked suspiciously. "Okay, fine. What were we talking about? Oh yeah, about Shuji being mad?"

"Yeah."

"He's not really mad, just frustrated. As far as I can tell, anyway."

"Frustrated?" I questioned, drawing my eyebrows together to make my feelings clear.

"Yeah. He's been practicing *Atafami* nonstop. Like, so much it's kinda freaky."

I was surprised—and hurt that she'd said practicing *Atafami* was "freaky."

"Really?" I said. Then I remembered another one of my topics. "After I beat Nakamura, I was sure he was gonna bully me in class."

"What? Why?" Izumi-san whispered. She was kind enough to smile. "Geez."

"Yeah, I'm still worried about it."

"You worry too much! I doubt that'll happen. I'm sure you'll be fine."

"Really? That's a relief," I sighed.

"Ha-ha-ha, good."

"Yeah."

Yes! Done! I survived! The conversation seemed over, so I figured I'd better quit while I was ahead for now so it didn't keep on going and reveal my lack of preparation. I had to do this twice a day until Friday, which meant seven more times. *Don't force it! Don't force it!*

After that, I got through all seven times, sometimes in a confused muddle, sometimes awkwardly, but I always pushed ahead with pure will. To be honest, the conversation about Nakamura was the longest one, and all the others were just barely enough to count as conversation. Frankly speaking, all seven were pretty close to a failing grade, and I'd say three or four were actual failures. Maybe only three, if you count this conversation as a pass: *"Oh, Izumi-san, are you wearing a different cardigan from yesterday?" "No, it's the same one..." "Oh, guess I'm imagining things." "Yeah."* *"..." "..."*

Yeah, I'm sure I passed. *Ha-ha-ha. Ha. I hate everything.*

"You passed."

"Seriously?"

We were in Sewing Room #2. I genuinely believed I must have failed, so this was a surprise.

"Yes. You completed the assignment of talking to her twice a day, so you passed."

"...Really? You mean it wasn't a problem that some of the conversations were terrible?"

"Nope."

An idea struck me. "So the point was to practice getting the nerve up to talk to someone!"

"Wrong."

"Huh...? So then, what?"

Hinami held up her fingers in a peace sign. "Do you know the two kinds of game overs?"

"That's a little random. Two types of game overs? ...What are you talking about? I have no idea."

"It's like this," she said, turning first her right then her left palm upward. "The kind where you go back to a save point and do it all over, or the kind where you do a retry starting from where you messed up."

"Oh, okay. Yeah, it varies depending on the game... So?"

"This week, you talked to Yuzu. These were like your 'battles.' You messed up, you were defeated, and then game over, right?"

"So I did fail."

"Obviously. A conversation that ends after three exchanges doesn't count as a conversation."

"…Oh r-right."

"So if you get a game over in a conversation battle, which kind do you think it is?"

"…I guess the kind where you do a retry."

"Correct. There are no save points in real life. On the other hand, even if you lose, you're not gonna lose half the money you have on you or anything. So there's no minus to losing a battle. Fighting as much as you can will benefit you. And with enough battles, you just might get lucky and win, right?"

"…Well, if you put it like that, I guess so."

"But that's not the really important point. Listen. There's one thing about failure in the game of life that's different from all other games… Do you know what it is?"

She grinned and peered into my eyes.

"Uh…that's so broad. Maybe…?"

Hinami interrupted my mental search. "I'll tell you," she said, then slowly explained. "In life, you get EXP for losing battles, not winning them."

"…Hmm."

I liked the sound of that.

"This week, you relentlessly fought Yuzu Izumi, a strong opponent, and lost repeatedly. But each loss became an experience point, and those points are building up inside you. You were thinking about the best way to go about it the whole time, right?"

"Yeah, I guess." I was a little happy she'd trusted that I'd done that.

"Honestly speaking, I think she got the impression that you're the weird guy who always talks to her."

"Really? I thought so."

"But you gained a lot, too. Didn't you notice it yourself? The further along you went, the more your tension dissolved and the mellower you got."

"Uh…I guess."

It was true. The conversations themselves were short, but especially the last two times, it was like…I don't know, like the weird vibe I've been emitting since I emerged from the womb had mostly disappeared. I mean, I'm not the one to judge, but anyway.

"Okay, so this week's exercise is over, now that you've practiced gaining experience points through defeat… Was there anything else you wanted to bring up?"

"Oh, um, yeah." Actually, there was. "You said Kikuchi-san liked me or something, right?"

"Yes, I did. And?"

"Well, I wouldn't say she *likes* me, exactly, but…I found out why."

Hinami stepped right up next to me. Super close. *Stop already, my heart is bad.*

"What do you mean?"

She was frowning, but her eyes were glittering with something like hope.

* * *

It was fourth period on Friday. I had one more conversation with Yuzu Izumi to go before I reached my quota. Since I'd already talked to her so many times, I'd gotten kind of used to it—or numb, maybe—so that whenever a conversation ended quickly, I figured whatever, I'd just try again. I'd been freed from my anxiety over the endeavor.

So I was fairly relaxed, thinking I'd be able to find some easy opportunity to make casual conversation, and I went to follow my usual routine before changing classrooms—that is, going to the library to kill time and then showing up in class just before it started. The only difference was where I usually pretended to read a book while I came up with strategies for *Atafami*, this time I was planning to review the conversation topics I'd memorized.

That's when it happened.

"Tomozaki-kun."

"Whoa?!"

I suddenly heard my name in a frighteningly clear voice. I turned toward the sound, and there, holding a book in both hands and peering at my face, was an angel of light—er, Fuka Kikuchi.

"…Oh, Kikuchi-san? What are you doing here?"

"Um, I'm always here…?"

"…Always?"

What did she mean? What was she talking about? A smell like a field of flowers in paradise was wafting from her and softly smothering my brain, making it difficult to think.

"You know…it's always just you and me in here when we have to change classes…"

"Um…always?"

"Yes…I mean…you never noticed?"

So… "…Oh, you mean…"

"You're always in here when we have to change classrooms, aren't you…?"

"Yeah, yeah."

"I always do the same thing, so I thought, *Oh, there he is again…*"

"Oh really? I'm sorry, I was probably distracted…"

…thinking about strategies for Atafami. When I glanced at Kikuchi-san, I noticed she was looking at the open book in my hands.

"…You like Michael Andi…?"

"Huh?"

"Huh…? Do you not? You're always reading his books…"

Oh right, the book I was pretending to read. I pretty much always sat in the same seat at the library and took a book from the end of the nearest shelf, so it would always be the same one… But I had no idea if I should tell her that, so instead I went and said, "Oh yeah, right. I mean, he's okay…"

What to do? Realizing I wouldn't be able to survive this conversation without understanding the gist of the book, I glanced down at its pages for the first time, only to find a string of words so undecipherable they must have been some kind of secret code. "*Ebi daite!*" was followed by "*Mozun lekuku!*" and then the same set of words once more. A shallow dip into this book would get me nowhere, unfortunately.

"I thought so...!" Kikuchi-san's eyes always had that magic sparkle to them, but now they were glittering especially bright. "I love Andi's books, too...!"

"Oh, y-you do?" *Crap, what do I do now?* "Wh-what a coincidence..."

"I know, it's amazing!" Kikuchi-san brought her hands together softly in front of her mouth. "It's just like *The Poppols and Raptor Island*, isn't it?"

"Uh, The Poppols...?"

"You know, Andi's book...oh, you haven't read it yet...? Makes sense, they don't have it at the library..."

"Huh? ...Oh, right! Um, I mean, I really want to but it's hard, you know, to...," I said, trying to fudge my way through. Kikuchi-san's eyes sparkled brighter, like Spirit Droplet had doubled their magical powers or something.

"Right! It's so hard to find that one!"

"Huh?"

"That book hasn't been reprinted since it was translated twenty years ago, so not many places have it. You'd think they would, considering it's one of his most important books...! I wish it was easier to find!"

She even latched onto the fact that I hadn't read it yet, wiping out my last escape route.

"Huh? Oh, right, yeah! I totally agree, ha-ha..."

"Uh, um...," Kikuchi-san began, apparently mustering her resolve. "I'm sure...I'm sure I can tell you," she whispered, like she was persuading herself of something.

Oh...uh-oh. I suspected she was about to reveal an important secret. I mean, that was definitely what would happen if this was a light novel or a porn game. I definitely sensed a flag, but in this case, it was connected to our relationship as Andi-whatever reading buddies. *Meaning I'd better stop her now...*but by the time that thought entered my head, Kikuchi-san was already continuing.

"Actually, I'm...writing a novel... It's very much influenced by Andi's work... If you're interested, do you think you could read it for me?"

"What?! A novel?! You're writing a novel?!"

The mental attack came from an unexpected angle, made especially powerful by a pair of eyes misty with the morning fog around a sacred tree.

"Yes... I'm sorry, I shouldn't have asked... It was such a sudden request... Sorry to trouble you..."

"No, not at all! I-it's no problem at all! I'd be happy to, very happy! That is, if you think I'm qualified!"

The words came out of my mouth before I could stop them, and Kikuchi-san lit up with a sunny smile. "R-really? Thank you! I'll bring it to you soon...!"

"Yeah, okay! Uh...thank *you*."

"Of course!" she replied in her clear and bubbly voice. "...I haven't shown it to anyone yet."

"Oh, you...haven't? Are you sure it's okay for me to read it...?"

As warm light filled Kikuchi-san's eyes, my spine shivered with guilty sweat. "Oh yes! I mean...you, of all people...oh no...um...it's a...secret, okay?"

Faced with the almost spellbinding way she presented the question, I found my head bobbing up and down in agreement as if I'd been brainwashed.

"Got it, of course. A secret."

"Well, see you," Kikuchi-san said simply, standing up. Just before she left the library, she turned toward me, and called back to me with a play-ful expression.

"Ebi daite!"

Ha-ha. I'm dead. No turning back now. Who cares? In for a penny, in for a pound.

"Mozun lekuku!"

When she heard my response, an unimaginable smile like a fountain of light rose to Kikuchi-san's delicate forest-elf face and illuminated the library. Then she delicately trotted out of the room.

I still had a few minutes before class started. I was in almost the same frame of mind as a few days earlier, when I ran away from Yuzu Izumi after our conversation to avoid revealing my true incompetence. All I could do was escape into my analysis in shock. *I've really gotten myself in trouble now. What do I do?*

* * *

"So that's what happened…"

I made sure to keep the part about the novel secret, but otherwise I explained the whole encounter to Hinami.

"Hello?! There is an insane amount of potential right there. You'll be reaching your mid-range goal in like a week."

She sounded bored. *Nuh-uh, no way.*

"Just wait a second. It's not like we're going to start dating because of this or something. I'd be tricking her. Anyway, she's not gonna want to date me just because we happen to like the same author. I don't even like her."

"I can't believe you would trick a girl into liking you and then say something like that."

"Hey, that's misleading."

"Not at all. There's a guy she's been noticing in the library for a while. She drums up the courage to talk to him, and the conversation goes unexpectedly well. She's having a really good time. What's more, at the end of the conversation, she exchanges the secret greeting from that book with him… Look, if she's not experienced with men, I wouldn't be surprised if she's fallen for you."

"Hold on, don't cherry-pick. I also made a fool out of myself blowing my nose in front of her."

"Could that be a secret just between the two of you?"

"Get serious, please."

"…Okay, that was a joke, but I'm serious. It might be an exaggeration to say she's fallen for you, but chances are that she now has a minor crush on you. I'm not certain yet, of course." Hinami's eyes were deadly serious. "Considering the situation, it would be much more unfair to her if you tried to run from the reality. You can't get away from this by beating yourself up and saying she'd never fall for someone like you."

…Honestly, it seemed totally impossible, which made it hard to think about this in realistic terms. But if Hinami was right, running away would be a crappy thing to do. Plus, there was the novel, which Hinami didn't know about. Taking that into consideration, the likelihood was even higher, wasn't it? But what was I supposed to do now? How should I approach this?

"Assuming, for the moment, that you're right…I'm an ass, aren't I?"

"Huh? Why?"

"For not admitting right then and there that I hadn't read the book."

"…What's so bad about that? You didn't intend to mislead her, did you?"

"No, but I ended up lying to her…"

"In that case, no need to worry about it. Obsessing over something unavoidable won't get you anywhere. That's what wimps do. The important question is what to do next."

"…Right. I guess I should fess up."

"Take her on a date."

"Huh?"

"I think you should ask Fuka-chan on a date."

"Uh, that's a really crappy thing to do."

"What's crappy about it? Listen. The fact that you both like the same author is just an opportunity. Human emotions are complex; that one thing isn't enough to make her fall for you. It's about how you talk, how you understand each other, how you create memories together. Even if there was a slight misunderstanding involved in how you met, that's not the core of the relationship. If you go on a date and end up having fun, and the author has nothing to do with it, that's a true sign of your compatibility, don't you think?"

"Uh…I—I guess."

"There aren't many opportunities for people to truly get to know one another. So even if it starts out with a lie, shouldn't you dive in if you're fortunate enough to find one?"

"I understand your logic, but…it seems insincere."

"If you understand my logic, then you can see I'm right, can't you? You sound like such a virgin."

"Shut up. That's because I am a virgin."

...I did understand what she was trying to say. Still, if you didn't think so logically for a moment, it felt insincere.

"...Fine. You don't want to fight with the strongest sword; you want to fight with the one you've been upgrading the whole time. I get that. The most logical choice isn't necessarily the correct one. In the end, I'm just your strategy book. You're the one who makes the final decision."

...I...

I left the sewing room that day still mulling over the question, which was anything but easy to answer. After Hinami and I split up, I was getting my shoes in the front hall when I saw Yuzu Izumi trudging toward me from the opposite direction. Uh, what to do? I'd already met the day's quota, so I didn't especially need to talk to her... But was only doing what I was told really the best gaming strategy? As the guy who prided himself on being Japan's top gamer, it bothered me. I didn't like the thought of leaving everything up to Hinami.

Okay then, I'm going for it: a self-motivated level-up.

Paying attention to my posture, expression, and tone, I called out to her as naturally as possible.

"Izumi-san?"

She flinched as if she'd been pricked and turned toward me.

"...Tomozaki...?" She sounded half disappointed, half reassured...not her usual self. Like she was spitting out my name. Speaking of which, I didn't recall her dropping the "kun" from my name before.

But all that aside... *Shit.* I'd memorized a bunch of topics, but none of them was urgent enough to justify calling out to her after school. God this was awkward. Once again, my mind was a blank. So awkward. *Think! I've practiced so much; I should be able to find a way out.* Something among all the strategies Hinami had taught me and all the effort I'd put in on my own.

If you can't think of anything, the other person can be the topic, like their expression or hairstyle.

Flashback. *Right. That's what Hinami said during out review meeting at the beginning of the week.* She'd told me to do that when I couldn't come up with any other topics. Maybe it would work right now. And her expression was...

"...Izumi-san, you look gloomy."

Oh come on, what did I just say? If one of the cool crowd had been here, they'd probably have come up with something like "What's wrong?" or "You can talk to me." Unfortunately, this was me. And I couldn't do that.

"What?! No, I'm not! What are you talking about?!"

"Oh sorry."

She was super-pissed. "...What are you looking at?"

"Nothing."

"..."

"..."

Did it again. Well, that's the end of that. I might as well give up on taking the initiative. Nothing's ever worked out when I took the initiative. I haven't even made it to beginner level. Of course not.

"...Um."

"Huh?"

"...Tomozaki, you're good at *Atafami*, right?"

"Huh?" *Why's she bringing that up now?*

"...me?" She was mumbling something as she stared at her shoes.

"...Huh? What did you say?"

"...me!"

"Sorry, what?"

"Oh, come on!" she shouted. When she raised her head to glare at me, I saw big tears pooled in her eyes. *What?!*

"I said, teach me to play *Atafami*!"

What on earth is going on?!

* * *

Here's the short version of Yuzu Izumi's story.

Until recently, she and Nakamura had been good friends and often left together after school. But recently, Nakamura had started setting up camp in an empty classroom every day after school to practice *Atafami*. Even when she went to the room and invited him to walk home with her, he told her, "Shut up and leave me alone." She offered to help him practice, but after he crushed her in their first game, he rejected her completely. ("Playing you isn't even practice. Anyway, you're annoying. Just stop following me around!") Or so she said.

"Huh. Fair enough."

Well, it's true, he wouldn't get much practice playing some random girl. After all, he wasn't bad.

"That's, um…that's rough."

"…I wasn't asking for your opinion!" she fired back, her cheeks flushed. "Anyway, are you going to teach me or not?!"

She seemed defiant, trying to make sure I knew she didn't care what I thought of this other side of her.

"I mean, I can, but…"

"What? You can?! Really?!"

She swiveled toward me, eyes flashing. She was super in my face. Why did Hanami and the other normies always get so close to people? Like, lethally close for us not part of that social class.

"But do you own *Atafami*?"

"Huh? Can't I use yours? I have a console."

"…Okay, that's fine, but…"

There was one major problem.

"…Where would we do it?"

"…!"

Yuzu Izumi opened her eyes wide and blushed. What was with the naive reaction? Very surprising.

"Yeah, we don't have a spot, do we?" she said.

Indeed we didn't. If she had the game, we could have played online, but since she didn't, we'd either have to play at her house or mine. Just the two of us, a guy and a girl.

"…But…!" Her expression was both pleading and determined.

"I mean, if we went to one of our houses, it would be…," I said.

"…Fine. No problem."

Her gaze was determined, but when I looked closely, I saw tears welling in her eyes. This wasn't easy for her. *She hates the idea of being alone with me that much, huh? That really hurts.*

"…That's fine, but…" I decided to ask her the question on my mind. "Why do you want to do it so badly?"

She turned on me angrily, or maybe she was just surprised. "Huh? You're really asking me that? Isn't it obvious?!"

"Obvious…?"

"Are you an idiot?! You really are dense! Ugh, freak!"

This generation really does like the word "freak."

"Dense…?" *Wait, I see what this is all about.* "…Oh."

"Huh? What?"

I finally got it, and the sudden rush of understanding escaped through my mouth, too. "So you have a thing for Nakamura!"

When I looked over at Yuzu Izumi, her face was so red I expected steam to come out of her ears any second.

"You really are a freak! It's unbelievable!!"

She whirled around, her necktie and skirt flying as she landed a clean hit on my face with her school bag.

"…Ow… So, um…"

"Oh, s-sorry…but you say such weird stuff! …Are you okay?"

Yuzu Izumi craned her neck around to peer worriedly at my downturned face.

"I'm fine, I'm fine," I assured her automatically, leaning backward. My voice was weirdly tense due to the extreme proximity of such a cute face.

"Are you sure? Um…but anyway! Shuji really doesn't get it. You know Erika? She told Shuji she liked him, but he turned her down. Erika! But he hangs out with me a lot…so I thought he might like me, but no! Apparently not. But anyone would assume he did, right? And then he suddenly goes and tells me to 'shut up' and 'not hang around him'… What the hell?! What do you think?!"

"Wh-what do I think? It…doesn't make sense?"

"Right! And on top of that..."

...He had her wrapped around his finger! Just like a character in some teen drama! Honestly, girls will gripe to anyone.

I thought about the situation as I sniffled through my throbbing nose. Yuzu Izumi kept on indignantly reeling off extremely personal complaints, but I didn't hear a single one. Instead, I was thinking about how much trouble I was in now. This girl was a genuine normie, no exaggeration. She was even friends with the one and only Nakamura, which gave her an extra strong claim to the title. Plus, she was cute and had big boobs. And the two of us were going together, alone, to one of our houses? *What is going on? This is so weird. Hey, Hinami, sorry for insulting you all the time, but what do I do here?*

"Um...which house should we go to?" I said.

"Uh... Can we go to your house? My house is...not great for this."

"Oh, my place...? Yours won't work?"

"Clearly! What would I tell my parents? ...Sorry."

"...Okay."

After getting angry for a second, Yuzu Izumi looked down and apologized. She wasn't so bad after all.

...Hey, wait... Parents? ...Uh-oh. That was when I realized something terrible.

"Oh wait. We can't go to my house. It has to be yours."

"What?! Why? You already said it was okay!"

"I did, but...Izumi-san, you play badminton, right?"

"Huh? Me? Yeah, but..."

"You know there's a first-year named Tomozaki, right? I mean, you two are friends, I think." I'd heard my sister mention Izumi-san a couple times.

"Uh, yeah, Zakki, right? I know her, but...wait. Tomozaki?"

"Yeah. She's my sister."

"...Whaaaaaaat?!" I tried to tell her she didn't have to act so surprised, but she talked right over me. "Wait a second! You guys are nothing alike! Especially your personalities! What?! I don't get it!"

"I know, I know. I feel like it's impossible for us to be related, too."

"I mean, Zakki is so cheerful and great! And you're so gloomy! What?! No way! That's so weird!"

"I already said I know! Stop talking about it already! I'm gonna get depressed!"

"...Oh s-sorry." As she calmed down, the problem dawned on her. "...Yeah, that wouldn't work."

"...Right?"

Of course it was. It would be way harder to explain the situation to a younger team member than to her parents.

"Um, well...that leaves my place..."

"...Yeah...guess we should just forge—"

"No, it's fine. Come over."

She looked at me with the peaceful expression of a girl ready to drink the poison. Yeah, women in love were strong, willing to suffer any hardship for the one they loved. Of course, I'd rather ignore the fact that this particular hardship was having me over to her house.

"...Oh."

"But are you sure you're okay with it, Tomozaki?"

I guess she was more sensitive to my mood than I'd thought. Ducking out was apparently a real option.

...What should I do? The only weapons I knew how to wield to some degree at this point were expression, posture, tone, and memorized topics. Would that be enough to clear the insanely difficult dungeon of Yuzu Izumi's house? Chances were slim to none. All that awaited me was a disgraceful defeat. In which case, I should escape. Escape. That's what I'd always done in the past. Fled from enemies I couldn't defeat, and fought again once I was better prepared. It was a tried and true tactic for video games.

"In life, you get EXP for losing battles, not winning them."

Another flashback.

Oh yeah, she did say that. Right. I didn't blindly believe her, but the fact was, at this very moment I was having a somewhat normal conversation with Yuzu Izumi. The old me could never even have imagined this. Maybe it was too early to conclude that the EXP and levels I'd gained by losing had led me to this outcome, but it sure seemed like a natural conclusion to reach. *Oh, geez. I get it already. I am a gamer after all.*

Hey, Hinami! Watch this. I'm about to test out your claim that losing results in experience points. I'm stepping right into a crushing defeat. Don't come crying to me when it happens!

"Yeah, it's fine. I'll go," I said, indifferent now that I'd decided to do it. "Where's your house?"

For some reason, Yuzu Izumi acted disgruntled. "…Tomozaki, why are you so calm? What? You've been to a girl's house before?"

"Uh, n…" I was about to say I hadn't, when Hinami's face floated before my mind's eye. "Oh yeah, I guess I have."

"Huh?! What? But you're…Tomozaki! Even I…even though…"

What was that supposed to mean, "You're Tomozaki"? Was she trying to say that because I failed so hard at life, I couldn't possibly have been to a girl's house, and if I had, it was gross? Okay, so I wasn't a normie, but that didn't give her the right to say something like that. And that's exactly what I told her.

"You keep using that weird tone of voice. It's freaking me out… Anyway, let's go. This way," she said.

"Wait, I have to go get the game."

"Oh right."

We went to my house, where I picked up *Atafami* and a couple of other things and went right back out.

"Okay, this way."

With that, she beckoned me toward the deadly dungeon. *Just watch me Hinami. I'm gonna get my butt kicked.*

* * *

Since Hinami's room was my only point of reference, I was naturally going to compare Yuzu Izumi's room to hers.

My first impression was that it was more cluttered. It wasn't especially messy, but there were a bunch of character plushies on her bed, and her desktop was packed with rows of what looked like fashion magazines featuring someone popular on the cover. Everywhere I looked was crowded, bright, and showy. Even I knew the names of the characters and magazines lying around, all of which seemed designed to attract buyers on the basis of fads. The walls were decorated with corkboards overloaded with carelessly pinned-up photos—both from photo booths and regular cameras—of our normie classmates. Must be her "BFFs," as they say.

"Tomozaki, you're staring."

"Oh sorry."

Yuzu Izumi came in carrying a cute mug and a regular paper cup on a round tray.

I stared at it. "…"

"Shut up! Don't complain!"

I wasn't complaining…

"So…what do I do?" Izumi said, gripping the controller, straightening her posture, and facing the start screen on the TV with laser focus. Her big, round eyes reflected the screen.

"Well, for now…," I began, sitting down far enough away that I wouldn't be suffocated by the normie aura and picking up the other controller, "should we have a match?"

"What?! No way! I mean, you're even better than Shuji, right?! No way can I play you!"

"I know, but…if I don't know what level you're starting out at, Izumi…"

I realized I'd naturally dropped the "san" from her name. I have no idea if it was because I'd grown through so many defeats, or because we were playing *Atafami*, or because she'd whacked me with her school bag and I just didn't care anymore.

"Oh, so that's how it works…? I guess it's okay, then…"

She looked very timid and nervous. Her shoulders were all scrunched up, her mouth was pulled tight, and her eyebrows were furrowed intensely. Strangely enough, it was a good look for her.

On the character selection page, I chose Nakamura's standby, Foxy, and Izumi chose a cute swordswoman, the showiest option available.

"Oh, hold on."

"What? Is this character not good?"

If Izumi's goal had simply been to master *Atafami* for fun, then using a character she liked would have been best. But her goal right now was to become Nakamura's practice partner. In which case...

"Use this one," I said, pointing the cursor at Found. "He's the one I usually use."

"Huh? Yours? Is it better?"

"No, but Nakamura's practicing so he can beat me, right? He probably wants to get ready to face my character. So..."

"Oh...I see." Izumi nodded gravely. "You're so smart, Tomozaki."

"Uh, r-really...?" I answered, embarrassed by the compliment. "...Anyway, are you ready?"

"Yeah!"

The mood was gradually becoming friendlier. Here I was in a girl's room, playing my favorite game, a situation in which only normies found themselves. I was overwhelmed by emotion at the thought of how far I'd come.

"...No way..."

Izumi was astonished.

"All right, I've got a basic idea now... First, what you need to work on is..."

"...Forget what I need to work on! What did you just do?! Your moves were super-freaky!"

We'd each started with four stocks, and the match ended without me taking any damage at all, let alone losing a single stock. As a result, the friendly mood of earlier had vanished. *How far I've come, huh? As if!*

"Well, you're doing the typical beginner moves. You blindly use techniques that leave you wide open, and you're not watching what I'm doing. I can take advantage of those openings to whale on you without even thinking about strats," I said, adjusting my imaginary glasses as I coolly enumerated her mistakes.

"Huh? What? Whatever you're saying, it's freaking me out."

Izumi was inching away from me, but I ignored her and continued with my analysis in a low voice.

"You did a surprisingly decent job with the most basic fundamentals, like the inputs for your specials and edge recovery, so...the problem is with your neutral game... You used too many specials, so if you use normal attacks more..."

"Hey, what are you talking about? You really are so weird!"

"Izumi!"

"Y-yes?!"

She gave a start, then switched from sitting cross-legged to tucking her legs under her, her back ramrod straight. She was very athletic.

"For now, I've figured out what I want you to do."

"Really?! What?!"

She leaned toward me, her eyes sparkling. Her face was super-cute, and her boobs were huge, and she smelled good. *Shit.* But I didn't see any of that when it came to *Atafami.* (Well, I was still aware of the nice smell.)

I selected training mode and showed her how to control her character.

"When you do a normal jump with the character you were just using, this is what happens."

Found leaped into the air. Izumi's deep black eyes followed him intently.

"But if you tap the button really lightly, this happens."

"...Oh, he doesn't jump as high."

Found had jumped about a third as high as he had before.

"This is called a short hop. When you really get into *Atafami,* it's about paying attention to your opponent's timing and moves, then fine-tuning when to leave yourself open and competing to see who can attack with the least risk. With the technique I just showed you, you can get your timing really precise, so it's essential to perfect it."

"W-wait a second!"

Izumi sprang up and trotted over to her desk, stumbling a little.

"Ouch! Pins and needles!"

She pulled open the drawer, took out a pen and notebook, and came back to her spot.

"…And?"

She jotted down what I'd just said, then looked up at me with an anxious but intent expression. She was definitely serious about this. She was sitting formally on her knees again, ready for instruction, which worried me slightly.

"Try it."

"O-okay…" She picked up the controller with extreme caution and tapped the jump button.

"Huh?"

"…Yup."

Found had jumped high into the air.

"W-wait! Let me try again!"

Boooing! Boooing! Boing! Boooing! Boing! She was getting it right about 30 or 40 percent of the time.

"Yeah, it's pretty hard. But if you can't do it, you probably won't be good enough to play Nakamura…"

"Not good enough…? Okay then, I'll practice!"

"Yes, but that won't work, Izumi."

"Huh?"

I wasn't stumbling over my words any more. This was my battlefield.

"Here, you can actually practice playing *Atafami*. You shouldn't be wasting your time on short hops. Practice the real deal, because you'll get more out of that."

"O-oh, really? …But what about the short hops?"

"Well, you do need to practice those. But when you're playing the actual game, it's more effective to practice in a real match. So what do you do? …There's only one answer."

I visualized a very familiar proud face and tried to mimic it.

"You should practice when you're not playing *Atafami*."

"Wh-what do you mean?"

"Well," I said, pulling something I'd made sure to bring along from my pocket. "You use this."

"…A stopwatch?" Izumi became even more confused.

"Yeah. Watch this." I pressed the button to start the timer running, then I clicked it again. "Look."

"…Huh? The timer didn't stop… But it definitely sounded like you clicked it…"

"…Now you try, Izumi."

"O-okay."

She took the watch from me delicately, as if she were handling a precision instrument. She pushed the start button, leaning her whole body into the motion, and then pressed it again.

"…Huh? …It stopped."

"Yep… This stopwatch is slightly broken."

I took it back and started the timer, then clicked the button again, showing Izumi the face of the watch. *Click, click, click, click,* over and over.

"Huh? It's not stopping."

"Right. If you don't press the button for long enough, it won't stop, even if it makes the clicking sound."

"Huh. Really? …But what do I use it for?"

"It's simple," I said, holding up one finger like a certain someone. "From now on, whenever you're going to school, moving between classes, or watching TV—in other words, whenever you're not with other people—I want you to practice pressing the button too quick for it to stop! Pretty soon you'll be able to do the short hops in no time at all!"

"Really?!"

She looked surprised, probably as much by my tone as by what I was saying. Whoops, I'd emulated Hinami's style a little too much.

"When you're doing other things, practice with the stopwatch. When you're at home where you can practice *Atafami*, practice actually playing. That's the most effective way to improve."

"That makes sense…! But why are you acting like you're my big sister?!" she said, carefully writing down my instructions in her notebook. She looked so silly I couldn't help wondering if she'd really understood, but she also seemed so totally convinced that I almost started laughing. About my tone, I simply hand-waved it with a "Don't worry about it, it was a mistake," and she nodded, satisfied. *Excellent. Disciples who listen make the best progress.*

"And as for practicing with real matches…that's easy, too."

Izumi gulped.

"It's all about memorization."

"M-memorization?"

"Yeah. Here, look."

I switched the game mode to replay, chose a game from the memory card I'd stuck into the slot, and started it up.

"This is a game between two top players that I saved."

"Um, nanashi? And NO—"

"Don't worry about the names. Usually both of them use Found, but in this game, nanashi was trying out Foxy, and the other player was using Found."

Izumi watched in shock, frowning intently.

"…Whoa. Their moves are as freaky as yours were earlier."

"Yeah, Found is a top-tier, no-BS kind of character. The player controlling him isn't going by feel like I—I think this guy nanashi does. They've used logic to refine their moves. That's why they make a good model to learn from."

"…So I'm supposed to watch this over and over and, like, remember it?"

"Close, but not quite." I handed Izumi the controller.

"Not 'like.' I want you to perfectly memorize this game from start to finish until you can use the controller along with it as you watch."

"…Are you serious?"

Dead serious.

"This match starts with four stocks for both players. Neither of the players gives the other many opportunities to attack, so it lasts over ten minutes. Memorizing it will be tough, but if you do, you'll have a feel for all the important techniques you need to play this game. I…um, I mean, nanashi tries out all kinds of fighting methods to explore what Foxy can do, and Found's responses are also really varied."

"O-oh."

I could practically hear Izumi's brain short-circuiting, but I hadn't completely lost her yet, so I continued.

"Once you've memorized all of Found's moves, move on to Foxy. Once you've memorized both, I think you'll be ready to play Nakamura."

"R-really?"

Her face broke into a truly joyful smile. *So this is the smile of a maiden in love.* I nodded.

"…But," Izumi said, her face clouding over, "I won't know how to use the controller just from watching the recording. Like, I won't know how to make them do the techniques…"

She was right. Even if she wanted to copy the moves, she wouldn't necessarily be able to… But the solution was simple.

"That's why I said 'memorize.'"

"Huh?"

Ignoring her confusion, I pulled some paper and a pencil box out of my bag and drew a simple diagram and table.

"…You're going to memorize this."

"What is it? …A table of techniques?"

"Yeah," I replied, filling in the boxes. "This column that says 'Command' tells you what button presses you do to deploy the technique. This stick figure shows the position the character will be in when you do it. The area inside the blue line shows about how far the attack reaches, and the red line shows where you're invincible. The 'Start-Up' column shows how long it takes after inputting the command for the first hitbox to appear."

"Um…"

Right from the start, she seemed lost.

"What does this 'F' mean…?"

"It means 'Frames.' In *Atafami*, the frames are 1/60th of a second. Just remember that the shorter it is, the sooner the technique starts. The 'Damage' column shows how much damage you'll do to your opponent. The 'Knockback' column shows how far they'll go flying. Pay close attention to that column because with some techniques more damage leads to more knockback, and with others it leads to less."

"Uh…okay!"

She sounded enthusiastic, but her face revealed that she was totally lost.

"Anyway, you don't have to understand it all right now. If you just memorize the game and this table together, you'll gradually get a sense of each technique and why the players used them when they did. Actually, you should be thinking about that while you're memorizing the match… But even if you just physically remember what to do, your level will go way up, so that's good enough."

"G-got it…," Izumi replied, finishing up her notes. "…But, like, Tomozaki, did you memorize everything in this table? You wrote it all out so smoothly. You didn't look at anything…"

"Huh? Oh yeah, of course."

Izumi seemed surprised by my answer, but I kept talking.

"I've perfectly memorized all the techniques for all thirty-eight characters, not just Foxy and Found."

"…S-seriously?"

"Yeah. Want me to write them down?"

Izumi's surprise turned to revulsion, and then to interest.

"It's amazing," she said, a curious look in her eyes.

"What is?"

"It's like…okay. I'm impressed, but…you've done all that, and you don't get anything in return, right? I mean, why put so much into it?"

What was she saying all of a sudden? Was this her way of putting me down for my geekiness?

"Huh? You're asking me why? I don't do it to make friends or get compliments, that's for sure."

To me, that much was obvious, but Izumi widened her eyes in surprise.

"Really?! But it's a game!"

"Of course. What do you think games are about, anyway?"

On second thought, our generation *does* play games to make friends.

"I mean, if you're that good, people avoid you. No one stands a chance against you, and it kinda put me off earlier, too. If you're just a really flashy player, people might act impressed. But if you go too far, they're gonna say you'd have to be a freak to be that good. I bet that sucks."

She looked strangely earnest. Right then, I remembered a similar recent conversation—the one I had with Mimimi when we walked home together. I think she was getting at the same thing.

"Well, it does kinda suck… But I set myself a goal to master the game. I'd hate to fail way more than I hate being avoided by everyone."

"Huh…really?"

I decided to ask her a question and confirm my suspicions. "You're asking if I don't care what other people think?"

"R-right!"

Just like I thought. Mimimi had said that she would bend for the sake of the mood or keeping things fun. As far as I could tell from our current conversation, Izumi seemed to be the same type of person. It was like a habit, part of her personality. Of course she'd approach gaming the same way.

It wasn't a coincidence; this seemed like proof of what Hinami said—that most people were this way. They had no solid set of values, so they were constantly questioning their unstable selves.

"It's not that I don't care…it's just that other things are more important, or…"

"But isn't it rough being an outsider? You must not have fun during breaks, or really at all. Actually, I've never seen you having fun at school."

"Aw, leave me alone!"

"Ha-ha-ha!"

For a second, the mood relaxed. Still, this could be a serious problem. I think.

"But laughing with your friends isn't all there is to life…"

Going along with everyone else, getting their approval, being part of the group, not being avoided… People went along with the values someone else created—in other words, with what Hinami called the "mood"—just to keep from being excluded, just to be part of something. For Izumi, it was probably her current definition of happiness.

"Huh. Wow… I could never have that thought. Why not, I wonder? I've been like I am forever, and even if I wanted to change, I couldn't… Argh, I'm sorry! What am I saying?! Forget it, forget everything I said! The point is, everyone is different! To each their own!"

She flapped her hands like she was trying to turn it all into a joke. She was smiling, but I could see tears in her eyes as she avoided looking at me. It was probably partly embarrassment, but there was something else in her expression, too, something that suggested this was a very significant problem for her.

That's when I started to wonder about something. Mimimi and Izumi both had the same problem, so why was only Izumi so upset about it? With Mimimi, everything seemed light, like, "I'm Tama's guardian angel!" or "Life's better when it's fun, so I'm happy with how things are!" But right now, Izumi seemed so lost and serious.

What in the world explained the difference?

Was Mimimi just better at hiding it?

Suddenly, I remembered something. After my conversation with Mimimi, something had felt off. I couldn't have explained why, but it had occurred to me that Mimimi seemed like the one who was being supported. Now I felt like I was starting to understand the reason for that intuition.

I think Mimimi really was getting more support from Tama-chan than the reverse.

I remembered their conversation in home ec.

"Thanks for earlier, Minmi."

"...What for? I didn't do anything."

That relationship.

"Hanabi's heart is always laid bare, which means it's poorly defended. Someone has to act as her armor. Someone has to come swooping in and fend off the attacks, or else her heart will get all torn up..."

That was Hinami's analysis, but it matched up with my own guess.

Tama-chan was definitely being supported by Mimimi. But more than that...

I think Mimimi found meaning in protecting Tama-chan—in the person she was rescuing. It was like a goal inside her, just like continuing to play *Atafami* for me, and aiming to be the best at a variety of things for Hinami. She found real meaning in that goal, and in its results. And that was why she didn't feel lost.

Izumi didn't seem to have anything similar. For her, there was no

meaning in swallowing her feelings to accommodate other people. Without any goal of her own, she was simply swept along. She probably had lots of friends, but I was certain none of them filled the place that Tama-chan did for Mimimi—of the person who gave real meaning to her act of bending. That was why she felt unsteady and lost and questioned herself.

Sure, this was the analysis of a novice founded on the events of a mere week, but it's what my experiences were telling me.

And those experiences led me to another thought. The point wasn't to get other people to compensate for what you lacked, or to dole out what you had in surplus. It was to use your own strength to compensate yourself for your own shortcomings, all by yourself.

"I think you can change."

"What?"

"I mean, if you still want to."

"What? Change my personality? No way, I can't do that! What are you talking about? I'm about to turn seventeen! It's too late! I'm done talking about this!"

To ease the tension, Izumi gave a fake smile so perfect you couldn't even tell it was fake. Without even seeing it in action, I knew it was the expression she used to fight her way through the battlefield of the classroom.

And then—I don't know how to explain it, but I put together my conversation with Mimimi the other day, what Hinami had told me about Tama-chan's strengths and weaknesses, and Izumi's attempt to hide her feelings that actually ended up revealing them, and then I considered all of it in my own way. I also remembered two things Hinami had said.

"Conversation essentially consists of telling another person what you're thinking."

"Apparently, you're good at saying what's on your mind."

If that was true, and that's what genuine conversations were, why not try telling Izumi what I was thinking? *If I'm gonna fight my way through this super-hard dungeon, I might as well get annihilated giving it everything I have.* That was more or less my attitude anyway.

"...I was like that, too. From the day I was born until now, actually. I had a personality that never changed. Or maybe more like a worldview."

"What?"

My suddenly serious tone must have caught Izumi off guard because her fake smile wavered a little. I'd consciously tried to make my voice sound as intent as possible, and I was surprised that it had worked, even slightly, especially with a normie. I continued my line of thought.

"To me, life is the worst kind of game. Life is absurd. High-tier characters profit, and low-tier characters are exploited. There are no principles worth mastering. It's just a game of chance. There's no point in pouring my time and energy into something like that, and there's no need to. That was my way of thinking."

"O-okay..."

Izumi's smile was steadily turning to shock.

"So even if I lost at the game of life—for example, people ignoring me in class, not having a girlfriend or even regular friends, having a low social status—none of that mattered. 'Cause the game was shit to begin with. On the other hand, *Atafami* was a great game, so it was way more meaningful to win at *Atafami* than at life. It was awesome, and most of all, it made me genuinely happy. My whole life, that's what I thought."

Izumi stared at me silently.

"But recently, I met another gamer who's kind of insufferable, but also just about as good as me. According to them, life's one of the best games of all time. To tell you the truth, at first I was like, *What are you talking about? If you're a gamer like me and you haven't even noticed how shitty the game of life is, we have nothing to talk about.* But in the end, they said a bunch of stuff that convinced me. I still don't fully believe it, but they do know their stuff when it comes to games, so for now I've decided to test it out. In other words, I'm trying to take the game of life more seriously."

Izumi blinked in surprise.

"I've been learning strategies and ways to practice, and putting in as much effort as I can, and along the way, something clicked... I hate to say it, but I'm almost sure it's true now."

The next thing I said wasn't directed at Izumi so much as at the gamer with the best work ethic, the most confidence, and the worst personality in the world.

*   *   *

"As a game, I don't know if life's god-tier, but at the very least, it's good! That's what I think."

Izumi opened her mouth wide and smiled.

"So it's not one of the best, then, huh?"

I smiled, too, naturally this time instead of consciously making an expression.

"Yeah, I'm not that convinced yet. And I don't say something if I don't think it's true."

"…Wow."

"…Anyway, I'd been thinking life was a shitty game for more than sixteen years, but given just a small opportunity, I've come this far. Pretty amazing transformation, huh?"

"Ha-ha-ha. Yeah, it is, isn't it? Ha-ha, you're funny."

No, don't "ha-ha-ha." I'm not done talking.

"Point is, it doesn't matter. It doesn't matter if your personality hasn't changed for years and years."

Maybe she realized what I was getting at, because she gazed into my eyes with surprise.

"So Izumi, if you want to change, I think you can."

I forced myself to return her gaze.

"…Even now. I'm positive."

And that's how my attempt to clear the super-hard dungeon ended: not in victory and not in defeat, but in an unexpected outcome—persuasion.

* * *

"Y-you really think so…?"

Izumi's eyes were shining. I'd finished saying everything on my mind, so I was back to my old self, the one who couldn't ad-lib conversations.

"Yeah, well, maybe."

Izumi burst out laughing. "Ha-ha, what's that supposed to mean? You're not very reassuring!"

"…Sorry."

Since I'd managed to have such a long, natural conversation here at Izumi's house, I figured my skills must have improved subconsciously or something. Nope. It was just my regular abilities: talking about *Atafami* and saying what I was thinking.

"…But…yeah…I think I'll give it a try."

"Huh?"

"I mean, practicing *Atafami*, and…seeing if I can stop worrying so much about what other people think… Like you said, you don't know until you try."

"…Really?"

"Yeah…oh, that reminds me," Izumi added, taking out her cell phone. "Give me your number. I want to have it in case I have questions."

"What?! It's not like I'm some expert on what other people think!"

"Not that! Questions about *Atafami*!"

"Oh right…"

We exchanged numbers as Izumi gave me a look like, *What is this idiot saying?*

"Okay!"

"Uh, um, well…I'd better get going." After all, I'd taught her what I could about *Atafami*.

"Okay—oh, don't forget the game!"

"Oh, no worries, that's a spare. The memory card is a backup, too."

"Spare? Backup?"

"…Never mind. It means I have another one at home."

"Really? But…if you'd lent me this to start with, couldn't we have played online…?"

"Oh yeah! That's true…sorry."

"Ha-ha. Right! But this way let us talk about a lot of stuff, so it's fine!"

"Ha-ha." It was nice enough of her to say that. "Okay, bye."

"Okay, take care! Oh, wait…um, uh—"

"What's up?"

"Oh…nothing. See you later!"

I left her house wondering what she had wanted to say. Less than five minutes later, a short text arrived from her.

"Thank you."

Just those two simple words, no emojis or anything. I guess that's what she had wanted to say when I was leaving. Huh. She was a normie, but in some ways she was easy for me to connect with.

Right away, I sent a message of my own.

A message to Hinami, that is, asking her how to reply.

* * *

"The sword you were carrying just happened to work against the boss's elemental weakness, and the shield you had just happened to resist the elements she used. A miracle, I'd say."

It was Saturday. I'd sent Hinami an e-mail briefly describing my encounter with Izumi, to which she'd replied by telling me to report to her in person. Thus our emergency weekend meeting.

"A pretty amazing one, too," I said, already tired of the huge parfait on the table in front of me. "Actually, I've been thinking about it, and it feels like things are going a little too well lately. There was the thing with Izumi, and the thing with Kikuchi-san, too. Are you sure you're not laying any groundwork behind the scenes, Hinami?"

Incidentally, for some reason we were meeting at a famous parfait place in Tokyo, instead of in Saitama. Hinami was calmly eating an weapons-grade sugary concoction made up of strawberries, banana, and melon drenched in whipped cream and condensed milk.

"What are you talking about? I'm not doing anything. You're the one who's laying the groundwork."

"Huh? Me?"

"Yes, you. I mean, if you didn't always go to the library between classes, and if you hadn't talked to Yuzu and borrowed a tissue from Fuka-chan, she wouldn't have talked to you in the library. If you hadn't crushed Shuji Nakamura in *Atafami*, and if you hadn't been talking to Yuzu Izumi every day for a week, then bumping into her when she was feeling down yesterday wouldn't have ended up with you going to her house. You've summoned all of this yourself through your own actions," Hinami explained, working her way through 80 percent of the parfait we had agreed to split half and half after she made me order it. She did have a good appetite. I had already had enough after my 20 percent. By the way, it was called a Peach and Whipped Cream Cheesecake Parfait, or something like that.

"Okay, that's true, but…"

"You're so stoic. You can give yourself a little more credit for your hard work, you know. I mean, of course you don't have to. As long as you can stay motivated."

I wondered how she managed to speak so clearly with her mouth full.

"Well…I do give myself some credit."

Hinami stopped eating. "…Really?"

She looked pleased, but maybe it was just because of the parfait.

"That's fine, then. So what do you think? Isn't improving your life through your own hard work a beautiful thing?"

She grinned and peered into my eyes. I didn't know what to do, so I looked away.

"…I guess."

"Huh. So you're shy about that kind of thing."

"Shut up."

"Whatever. Anyway, your mid-range goal just got a little closer."

"…Did you even hear what I just told you? The reason Izumi is doing all this is because she likes Nakamura."

"All the same, I doubt she's ever had a deep conversation with Shuji like she did with you yesterday. Plus, you have something she doesn't. Okay, that's probably not enough to make her fall for you. At least, not *this* you."

"*This* me?"

"You may have grown a little, but you still have a lot to work on. In the long run, though, if you keep up the hard work and move forward step by step, it's not at all out of the question that something would happen this year."

"Seriously…?"

With Yuzu Izumi? The normie? Well, the fragile normie, that is.

"Yeah," Hinami said, polishing off the parfait. "I'm talking possibilities, of course."

"I can't believe you ate that whole thing…"

"Anyway, have you decided yet? About Fuka-chan?"

"Uh, I'm still going back and forth. But I'm almost there."

"...Huh. Well, I won't ask what you've decided. Tell me after you do it," she said, taking out her wallet. "If you do decide to ask her out, use these."

"...Movie tickets?"

"Yes. They're for a premiere of the new Mari Joan film next Sunday."

"A premiere? ...You think I should invite her to a movie?"

"Yeah, that's part of it. But the bigger thing is the first time you ask her out, you shouldn't come on too strong. With these tickets, you can act like someone gave them to you and you don't have anyone to go with. Since they're for a specific day, she can say she already has plans if she doesn't want to go. Plus, if you do end up going together, you don't have to talk as much, and afterward you'll have something in common to talk about, right?"

"Oh, okay..."

"Also, if she's really into you and she genuinely can't make it that day, it's very likely she'll suggest that you go out another time. All in all, it's a low-risk proposition."

"Huh... Well, I haven't made up my mind yet, but I'll go ahead and take them. Thanks."

"Sure," she said, standing up with her wallet in hand. "Sorry, I have to get going. I have a lot to do today. Since I ate most of the food and you had to pay to come all the way into the city to meet me, I'll get the bill."

I thought about protesting, but I knew that once she'd made up her mind she hardly ever changed it, so instead I thanked her meekly and left it at that.

* * *

That night, I was using the recorder Hinami had given me to tape my voice, play it back, and practice my tone, as I always did. But as I was trying to play it back, I accidentally pressed the wrong button.

"Oh shit, what's going on? Did I just switch folders?"

The file number should have read 63, but instead it read 781.

Uh-oh, how do I get back?

Suddenly, as I started pushing a bunch of buttons, a file started playing. *Shit! I probably shouldn't be listening to this without her permission!* As that thought ran through my head, I started to press the STOP button, when my hand froze. The first thing I heard caught me off guard.

"That's why Shimano dumped you! She's like... Younger guys are so... No, that's not right."

What the...?

"Younger guys...shoot! You just...aaah! ... Younger guys are soo...damn!"

It's what she'd said when she came to rescue me and Mimimi and Tama-chan in home ec.

"That's why Shimano dumped you! She's like... Younger guys are sooo immature...there! Younger guys are sooo immature! Younger guys are sooo immature! ... Got it!"

The recording ended.

I do have some respect for people's privacy, so I didn't consider listening to another file. But what I'd heard was enough. More than enough. Why was this girl amazing? I'd sensed it vaguely before, but now I knew without a doubt.

The amazing thing about her was how hard she worked to make herself that way.

* * *

The following week, on Monday and Tuesday I chatted casually with Izumi about *Atafami* during all our breaks. Nothing much happened aside from a few surprised looks from other people. Izumi was memorizing the techniques way faster than I'd expected. At this pace, she'd probably be able to play Nakamura before the week was out. When I told her as much, she seemed extremely happy. I'd found myself a good student. Plus, talking to her was easy since she sat next to me.

Hinami and I didn't talk about much in our strategy meetings. She just told me to keep diligently working on my posture, facial expressions, tone, and topic memorization, along with talking to Izumi and Kikuchi-san as often as possible.

And then Wednesday came—the most momentous day since I first met Hinami.

6

Sometimes you conquer a dungeon
only to find a strong boss back in your village

Today, one of our classes was in another room. Which meant that when I
went to the library before that class, I'd come face-to-face with Kikuchi-san.

I'd been talking to Izumi since morning about *Atafami*, and now it
was time for the break before we moved to the other classroom. I headed
for the library as usual, but not in my usual state of mind.

When I opened the door to the library, Kikuchi-san was already there.
She noticed me and gave me a smile like a soothing spring breeze. *She's
beautiful.* Then her gaze swept back down to the book she was reading. It
would have been easier if she'd started talking to me about Andi-whatever
again, but it looked like this time I'd have to make the first move. So as
not to startle her, I intentionally made some noise as I walked over. When
I was very close, she turned toward me with an impossibly graceful move-
ment, like some sort of sacred dragon.

"Hey... Is something wrong...?"

As it always did, her voice entered my ears like the splash of an angel's tear.

"Uh, I wanted to talk...," I said, pulling over the chair next to her so
it was an appropriate distance away before sitting down. If the sacred aura
of a beautiful girl envelopes a genuine social outcast like me at close range,
his body will dissolve in the light and evaporate.

"What's the matter...?" she said.

"Um..."

I know her eyes are pure black, but for some reason they appeared to
be a deep green imbued with elf magic. Before them, my resolve wavered.

"It's about that writer we were talking about the other day, Andi?"

"Oh, yeah...!"

Her eyes lit up. But I'd made up my mind.

"Actually…" I was determined to tell her point blank. "I lied when I said I liked that author. I mean…I haven't even read those books!"

"What…?"

To my surprise, Kikuchi-san was able to produce not only the aura of a fairy or an angel, but also that of an innocent young child.

Still I soldiered on. "It's true."

"What…? But I saw you reading…"

It was a natural question. If you saw someone sitting in the library with a book open in front of them on a regular basis, it was a normal conclusion to draw. But you would be wrong.

I told her how much I love *Atafami*, and how I spend my free time on it, and that the reason I come to the library is because I don't like the atmosphere when I get to the other classroom early…that I was just pretending to read books while I was actually planning out strategies for *Atafami*.

"So the truth is…I don't have any particular interest in that Andi person, and I haven't read any of their books. But I didn't know how to explain all that, so I just went along with what you were saying."

Kikuchi-san's expression was not condemning or forgiving—purely disappointed.

"Really? But what about the secret greeting…?"

"The secret greeting…? Oh! Ebi-whatever?"

"Yeah, it comes up a lot in the book you were reading that day… It's what they say instead of 'good-bye,' or 'let's meet again…'"

"Oh, they say it a lot? That makes sense, because it was written on the page I opened to. I blurted it out to keep from letting you know."

"Oh, I see…"

"Yeah, so it seems wrong to me—letting me read the book you wrote. Your offer was based on a misunderstanding…well, on my lie, really… I'm sorry."

"Oh…yes, I guess that's true." She let out a long breath. "Please don't worry about it."

She smiled forgivingly, washing clean my guilty conscience. I might have been getting ahead of myself, but I'd say she looked a little lonely, too.

I had to decide what to do next. I hadn't made up my mind until right before I got to the library. Now that I'd apologized, should I invite her to the movie or not? I brushed my hand over the tickets to the premiere in my inner pocket.

"…But," I added, conscious of my heart pounding. "I'm sure I'll come to the library again, so…next time, I thought maybe we could have a normal conversation about something else. Maybe not our favorite authors or anything. Also, I want to try reading some of Michelle Andi's books… What do you say?"

Kikuchi-san responded to my proposal with a few blinks her long eyelashes. Then she giggled cheerfully, like an ordinary girl our age instead of her usual fantasy-story self.

"…Ha-ha-ha! Tomozaki-kun. It's not Michelle—it's Michael! …You really haven't read his books, have you?"

"Oh… Michael. Uh, ha-ha."

"He-he."

"B-but, um, is it still okay…for me to come here?"

Kikuchi-san smiled a warm, heartfelt smile, like sun filtering through trees.

"…Of course it's okay!"

Her smile made me feel shy all of a sudden. "Good, okay, bye," I said quickly, leaving the library behind.

From there, I headed quickly to the home-ec classroom.

I thought it would have been unfair to invite her to the movie right then. I'd only just told her I'd lied, and she might still have some lingering excitement from thinking we shared a favorite author. It wouldn't be fair to ask her out until that excitement had completely disappeared and we were on even ground again. It would have been an insincere thing to do, and I'm glad I didn't.

*   *   *

Having sorted out the situation with Kikuchi-san in my own way, I felt more at ease for the rest of the day. Izumi and I had gotten into a routine of chatting a little about *Atafami* between classes, after which she joined the normies by the back window and I stayed alone at my desk. My confidence was rising, and I felt like I was making progress.

Of course, that's always when something has to go wrong.

* * *

"Tomozaki."

"Huh?"

Class was done for the day. The voice saying my name wasn't one I was used to hearing talk to me.

When I turned around, I saw Nakamura's buddy Takei glaring at me with his arms crossed. Mizusawa was standing stoically next to him like an impassive observer. It was the pair who hung out with Nakamura in home ec.

"C'mere."

"What?"

What was up? Was I being "summoned," as they say? If these two were doing it, Nakamura was definitely involved. But why? Hinami had let the air out of the balloon when it came to the *Atafami* incident. Had I done something to upset Nakamura? Or maybe this wasn't a negative summons at all? Fat chance of that, considering their tone.

"Just come with us."

Protesting probably wouldn't get me anywhere; following them was my only option. I glanced around the classroom to see if Hinami was watching, but she wasn't anywhere to be found... Maybe she was already in Sewing Room #2. Guess I'd be relying on my own strength to get through this sudden boss fight.

They led me—more like dragged me, really—to an empty room across and a little down the hall from the staff lounge that used to be the principal's office. Traces of its former identity—an old but still usable sofa and desk, a CRT TV—still remained.

Nakamura was there, along with a couple other normie guys.

"…Uh…?"

Including Takei, Mizusawa, and Nakamura, there were six of them altogether. *What the hell? Am I about to be lynched or something?*

"Hey, Tomozaki."

It was Nakamura. Just hearing him say my name was intimidating. I reflexively looked away and happened to see something familiar. *Huh? A console.*

"Hey, wait a second. Is this about *Atafami*?"

I didn't know how to react to this unexpected development. *Does he want to get his revenge by playing me again?*

"Sure is. Sit there."

I sat down in front of the controller he'd gestured to. The console switched on, and the familiar start screen appeared on the TV.

"Wait a second, what's going on?"

Nakamura's crew ignored my confusion and lined up at a distance from us, toward the back of the room.

"Exactly what it looks like," Nakamura growled. *I see.*

"So you want a rematch."

Nakamura clicked his tongue softly. "You sure are full of yourself," he snapped.

"Honestly, though…"

I glanced behind me. We had an audience. Meaning there would be witnesses to whatever happened. The last time we played, I'll be honest, I beat him so bad it was embarrassing. Most likely, the only people who knew that were me, Nakamura, and Hinami. I wouldn't be surprised if everyone else thought I'd won by a narrow margin.

But this match was going to be different. There would be witnesses to every last detail.

True, Nakamura might have practiced a lot over the past few weeks. Given his existing ability, that extra practice probably meant he could easily beat every one of the guys in the back of the room without losing a stock.

But I was another story. I was just too good. No matter how much he practiced in that short period of time, it would be a drop in the bucket.

Plus, I was confident I'd improved more than him since we last played. If I genuinely, truly avoided any risks and didn't worry about how long the battle went on, I could most likely avoid damage completely. Even if I didn't do that, beating him with four stocks would be easy.

Which meant we shouldn't be playing each other to start with. This would be more than a little embarrassing for him. Maybe if I could hold back on purpose, but when it comes to *Atafami*, that's something I just can't do. This was not a good idea.

"You shouldn't do this," I said.

"Seriously? You're that cocky?"

I'd glanced at the peanut gallery as I spoke, so he probably took my words to mean *"You'll embarrass yourself."* Once again, I'd pissed him off. Of course I had. Sugarcoating was way too advanced for me at this stage.

"No, I'm being serious. I know you've been practicing every day…but still…"

I stopped mid-sentence. I'd only piss him off more if I continued: *…it won't make up for the difference in our levels.* I'd already implied it, though, so it was probably too late.

…But his next question surprised me.

"Who told you I was practicing?"

I'd never heard him sound this intimidating. *Huh? Why's he asking about that?*

"Uh, Izumi," I said. There wasn't any reason for me to hide her identity.

"…Figures," he said, frowning. "Seems like you guys are friends now."

"Huh?"

…*Wait a second.* It was too soon to be sure, but wait a second. Logically, he shouldn't want a rematch yet, so I'd been wondering if there might be some other reason he'd called me here. *You don't think he…?*

"Why are you friends with Yuzu? Sounds fishy to me."

Yup, I was right. Hard to believe he'd said that so boldly in front of all those guys. *Okay, let's stop messing around here, Nakamura. The reason I talk to Izumi all the time is because she wants to go out with you, and that's why she's working so hard to get better at* Atafami. *I'm helping her get you. I'm Cupid's arrow in this scenario.*

And now you're picking a fight because you're jealous I'm friends with Izumi. Why do I have to put up with this?

"We're not really friends."

"What, then?"

I couldn't tell him the truth. Only a true asshole would out a girl in love to save himself. I might be inexperienced, but even I know that much. I had to use my skills to get out of this.

"No, it's just, we shouldn't play here. We should play at your house or mine."

"House…? Speaking of, you went to Yuzu's house, didn't you? Someone told me they saw you."

Seriously? I'd just woken another sleeping dog? I was done for.

Think about it. Some super-geek crushes you at a video game, acts cocky as hell, then befriends the girl you like—or maybe don't like? Anyway, they become friends and he goes to her house. Yeah, you'd be pissed. There was no getting out of this one.

"Um, it was more complicated than that…"

"Explain."

"…Uh, sorry, I can't talk about it…"

I couldn't think of a lie, and he must have interpreted my answer as *"It's a secret just for Izumi and me."* He got even more upset, clamped down his grip on the controller, and snarled, "We're playing. Now."

But social awkwardness is my specialty, and I hemmed and hawed and wasted time saying things like "But…" and "Come on" and "No…" and "I don't like the way you said that," hoping something might change in the meantime. I was praying for Hinami. It should be easy enough for someone like her to get suspicious when I didn't show up in Sewing Room #2, gather some information, and come galloping to my rescue. If I just killed enough time, I was sure she would come. I knew what she was like.

As I fervently prayed for Hinami and spun my wheels with nonsensical comments, the door to the room opened with a bang. *There is a God!*

"Sorry to interrupt y— Huh?! Tomozaki?!"

RIP lol, as they say. It was Izumi. *I can't believe this.*

"Why are you here, Yuzu? I told you not to come around."

"Oh sorry, Shuji. I just thought I might be ready...to play...you..."

She must have sensed the tension in the room, because the excitement suddenly drained from her voice. *Sorry, Nakamura, this really is the worst situation possible for you. I'd told Izumi she might be able to play you before the week was out, and then I'd been killing time until she got here. This really is all my fault. I should have played you right off the bat. Now that Izumi's seen you, you can't back out, can you? Is there any way you can let me go?*

"Whatever, it's fine. You can watch us play."

"Um, okay...!"

Damn. He'd done it. It was really over now. Izumi joined the guys lined up in the back of the room.

"Yuzu, come on. I told you it's not gonna happen. Let's go home."

The door opened for a second time, and in came Erika Konno, the girl Izumi had told me about, and her crew. Even among a group with bright, bleached hair and short skirts, Erika Konno stood out.

"Huh? What's going on?" one of the girls said.

"I'm gonna play Tomozaki right now. Watch me," Nakamura told her.

Oh geez. Erika Konno and her battalion filed in, joining Nakamura's crew. What was this? Super Attack Families Normie All-Star Mode or something? Why was he so intent on self-destruction? *Well, he's on his own now.*

"Let's go, Tomozaki. Can't run now, can you?"

"Fine," I sighed, steeling myself. Like I said, I can't hold back when it comes to *Atafami.* "...But you're the one who can't run, Nakamura."

In more ways than one.

* * *

Up till now, Nakamura had been the only person to experience how scathing I could be when I got cocky, but now a murmur rippled through the gallery. "Whoa!" "He doesn't hold back!" "That *is* Tomozaki, right?!" "This is getting intense!"

I wish they'd all shut up. I didn't care. If I have to do it, I'll do it and do it right. This is my art. *Hate yourself for picking a fight with me over* Atafami, *Nakamura. When it comes to this game, I'm A-tier.*

"Still as sassy as ever, huh, Tomozaki?" Nakamura whined. He was obviously mad.

I don't care. If you're gonna hit me, go ahead and hit me. If that's enough for you, great. But if we're gonna do this, let's do it and be done with it.

"Come on. Are we playing or not?" I coldly shot back, not looking at Nakamura as I picked up the controller. I'd had enough. Once we started, I'd let the sum of all my experience take over. I'd jump on the barrel at the headwaters and ride the river all the way to the ocean. I didn't need logic. My experience would automatically draw out the possibilities and carry me to the right one.

"Of course we're playing. Hurry up and choose your character."

Before he even finished talking, I'd chosen my usual character, as if this was just another match.

Tch. From my position near Nakamura, I heard him give an angry click of his tongue. Right. He was choosing his character. Foxy, as usual. Let's go.

I dashed toward Nakamura the instant the battle started. He started with a short hop and hit me with two long-distance projectile shots. Pairing the landing from a short hop with a ranged attack is a technique for eliminating the vulnerability after firing. Last time we played, Nakamura wasn't able to use such a subtle technique. He really had been practicing. But it was nowhere near enough to stop my flow. Without hesitation, distress, or any loss of focus, I let the current of my own knowledge sweep Found along. It was time to style on him.

I don't care if you can do a little more now that you've practiced, Nakamura. It's irrelevant. For you, it may be an earthshaking development, but from my perspective, you might as well have done nothing. It's like telling me, "Hey, I heard a species of ant in some African country evolved wings and now it can fly." Really? Huh.

You might have tried a new strategy on Found when he rushed toward Foxy, but it's about to be destroyed by my skill and experience.

As he approached, I wavedashed away with perfect timing five times. *Gachachachachacha.* There was no way he'd be able to respond to a move this insane and beyond his range of knowledge. I grabbed Nakamura, who was wide open, and comboed him all the way to KO. One stock down.

"What the hell was that?"

"His moves are so freaky."

"No way!"

"Huh?!"

The peanut gallery was in chaos. *Sorry to tell you, guys, but that's gonna happen three more times, and then this match will be over.* Of course, I wouldn't do five wavedashes in a row again—that only worked as a surprise attack with some extra flair.

The paths I could take next came into view of their own accord. There were seven or eight of them, like flashing channels of light. *Which one should I choose? Guess I'll go with this one.*

I intentionally started my dash attack slightly late, continuing the tiniest bit past Nakamura's block before stopping. He'd stepped forward, totally exposed, and he reached out to grab me right there. *Too bad. I passed you, so I'm right behind you now.* The grab left him wide open, so I turned and grabbed him instead. Then I threw him. Another combo. Second stock down.

"What?"

"He couldn't escape?"

"Is it just over once he grabs you?"

"That was sneaky."

"No way."

No, you *can* escape. If you're good enough. Nakamura was rattled now, and he wasn't using his controller well. Which left me with an infinite number of options. *Flash, flash, flash.*

They were so bright, and so many of them, too. *Guess I'll go straight ahead. If I take time choosing one, my eyes are gonna start hurting, and Nakamura's going down no matter which one I choose.*

I launched a simple dash attack. He blocked and grabbed me.

"Oooh!"

"He grabbed him!"

The peanut gallery was buzzing. It was the first time one of Nakamura's attacks had succeeded. He was probably planning to do a combo—guess he didn't know better. Yes, Foxy can start a combo from a throw when Found hasn't taken any damage, but only if the Found player sucks at DI—directional influence: the control that a player has over their character's knockback trajectory once they've been hit. If the Found player can use DI well, then the opposite thing happens—Foxy becomes vulnerable to a combo from Found. I guess you wouldn't realize that unless you'd practiced with someone who did it to you. Blame the situation, man.

Boom. Third stock down.

"…" "…" "…"

The peanut gallery was silent. No surprise there. The first two times, I took Nakamura's lives by starting with a throw and killing him with one combo. Finally, this time around, they think, "Wow, he grabbed Tomozaki!" But the very next instant Nakamura's getting stomped. At this point, the only thing left was cleanup. Easy. Routine stuff. The channels flashing in front of me were spread across a wide-open field. No matter which direction I walked in, I'd reach my destination. I leaped upward, and it felt like I was flying as my body floated and danced through the air. When I looked down, I saw an extraordinarily complex path stretching off toward the right of the field. Since I'd end up in the same place no matter what direction I went in, I figured I might as well get some practice in. Why not take that one?

I ran toward Nakamura and did a short hop. Back air. Right wavedash. Neutral attack. Short hop. Up air. Land. Jump. Slight neutral B charge, fire in midair. Land. Dash to where Nakamura just landed and grab him. Down throw. Jump. Forward air. Forward air. Double jump. Down B. Land. Neutral B charge. Jump. Double jump. Down B. Up B. Land. Short hop. Fire the neutral B. Dash. Run off the ledge. Forward air. Double jump. Down B spike.

Fourth stock down.
Game over.

* * *

Whew. Now I'd done it. To get through that high-pressure situation, I genuinely focused on the game, and as a result I completely destroyed him.

"...Shit," Nakamura muttered, like he was holding back his anger and distress. The peanut gallery watched in utter silence. With good reason. He'd been defeated in a four-stock game without taking a single one of mine. There was no way to explain it except that I was just that much better.

When I took his first life, people were saying things like it was creepy how good I was, but probably because Nakamura looked so deadly serious, they had fallen silent now.

I glanced toward the back of the room. Aside from Erika Konno, no one was looking at us. They were either exchanging awkward looks with one another, smiling in an attempt to ease the tension, or staring at the floor. *Sorry, Nakamura. But I didn't have a choice. I really didn't want to do it!*

"Well, I guess I'll be going," I said, hoping to escape the incredibly uncomfortable room. But three unexpected words stopped me in my tracks.

"One more game."

The person who spoke was none other than Nakamura.

What the hell was he saying? One more game? After what just happened? He couldn't be serious. It was impossible. No exaggeration, if we played a hundred times, he wouldn't win once. There was absolutely no reason for him to play me again.

"Uh, but..."

"I said, 'one more game.' Pick up your controller already."

"...Um, I want to change characters."

"No, it's fine like this. I'll keep mine, too. I'm not blaming it on the characters, so don't make fun of me."

"…Fine."

Nakamura didn't so much as glance at the peanut gallery. He kept his eyes fixed on the screen as he spoke. Everyone behind us was staring at the back of Nakamura's head in shock, and just a slight hint of fear.

I had no choice but to pick up the controller.

My brain wasn't on fast-forward like it was in the first match, so I took a little more damage, but once again, I beat him without losing a single stock.

Of course I did. I looked back at the audience. Among all the down-turned faces, I saw Hinami's. *Shit.* She must've slipped in during our second game. She and Izumi were whispering to each other, probably getting Hinami up to speed.

But I doubted that even Hinami could fix this situation. I didn't see it blowing over unless either Nakamura or I became the villain condemned to die.

When Izumi finished talking, Hinami seemed extremely troubled. Then she looked at me and shook her head.

I don't know exactly what she meant, but it certainly wasn't anything good. My situation probably wasn't going to improve much.

"One more time."

…I couldn't believe it.

He'd announced in front of practically every important member of the normie group that he wanted revenge, and then he'd lost two games in a row. Why hadn't he lost heart yet? *What is going through your mind, Nakamura? Why do you still want to fight?*

"Hurry up."

Apparently, my own opinions didn't matter.

"…Fine."

For the third time, I won without losing any stocks.

The mood was getting heavier by the second. If even I could feel it, those sensitive normies must be ready to suffocate. I looked back. Everyone except Erika Konno and Hinami was looking down. Under normal circumstances, I'd say they were being melodramatic. Hinami's face was blank. Erika Konno was glaring at us harshly.

"...I've got cram school today...," one of her crew said, attempting to leave.

"Oh, me too...," another one chimed in.

"Stop lying. You two have cram school on Wednesdays." Nakamura hadn't turned around, but his tone was still intimidating.

"Uh, well..."

"Ha-ha..."

And then—

"One more game."

You're lying, right Nakamura? Why are you doing this?

But there was no way I could talk him out of it.

"...Fine."

Again I full-stocked him.

Nevertheless.

One more game, one more game, one more game—three more times. The mood was like lead weighing us down, but Nakamura didn't change his attitude at all. Finally, in the last game, I lost one life before winning. And I swear I didn't hold back.

Great! That should satisfy Nakamura's thirst for revenge somewhat. Failing to KO your opponent even once over the course of so many games would cause more than a little damage to your pride; I get it. *So...*

"Nakamura, let's..."

"One more." He was staring fixedly at the screen.

"No, I'm done."

"Did you think I'd be satisfied with one life? I told you not to make fun of me. One more round."

For the first time since we started playing, he moved his gaze away from the screen and looked at me. There wasn't the slightest glimmer of self-doubt in his eyes; he was ready to fight. Apparently, this was more than mere stubbornness.

"...Fi—"

"Hey Shuji, give it up already, okay? I'm starting to think you're a geeky weirdo yourself."

*   *   *

I looked over my shoulder. The voice belonged to Erika Konno.

"I mean, come on. Why are you getting so serious about a game? It's dumb."

Nakamura turned his piercing gaze on Konno. "…What's it got to do with you?"

"What? You stop me when I'm trying to go home and tell me to watch, then say it's none of my business? Seriously? I don't actually think you're insane, but you're sure as hell acting like a creep," she scoffed with a mocking laugh. Nakamura's big show of intimidation hadn't had the slightest effect on her.

"I don't remember stopping you. Why are you following me around anyway, Erika? That's what's creepy."

Her face contorted.

"Wow. You sure are full of yourself. You think you're hot shit 'cause I said I liked you the other day? God, what a freak. Congratulations on misinterpreting everything. I only said it because I thought I'd be lucky to go out with the guy at the top of the pecking order. I'd never, ever have said it if I knew you were such a weirdo."

She sounded giddy, but her words cut like a sword.

"I couldn't care less what you think. Doesn't change the fact I don't like you," Nakamura said.

Erika Konno scratched her head with her pointer finger uncomfortablly.

"I mean, you can play him a million times; you're not gonna win. He's so much better than you it's hilarious to watch. If even I can see that, you must be pretty bad, huh, Shuji?"

"…"

For the first time, Nakamura hesitated. Swooping in for the kill, Konno turned to one of her crew for confirmation.

"Right, Miho?" Her timing was cruel.

"Uh, yeah, it's so weird. Like, I wish he'd just go home." The girl's contempt sounded completely heartfelt.

"Right? …Anything else?" Erika Konno was fanning the flames. I could hardly believe the techniques she was using.

"Uh, yeah, I mean, Nakamura's so lame to start with. Seriously, I wish he'd die."

"Right?!" Erika Konno crowed.

That was the cue for the rest of her crew to lay into Nakamura. Izumi was silent.

"He told us to watch him get his revenge, remember? What an idiot."

"Totally! Now look at him. It's insane. I want my time back!"

"Hear that, Shuji? You're lame and weak, and you always have been. You. Lost. Get it?"

Erika Konno's abuse was one level harsher than all the rest.

"What's it to you? Go home, then. Hurry up, get out of here."

Even Nakamura's verbal arsenal was withering under her force.

"What's it to me? That's funny. Hey, wait a second, is that a tear I see in your eye, Nakamura?"

"Oh my god, it is! What? He's crying? How old are you?"

"You're crying because you lost a video game? Are you kidding? You're not in preschool! I mean, I heard you've been practicing in here every day after school lately. Ha-ha-ha, you idiot. This is the best you could do? All your work was pointless. I'd be so embarrassed if I was you. This game is bullshit."

With that, Konno gathered her crew and made for the door. Hinami watched, moving her lips so slightly only I could have noticed.

But just a second before that, the voice of a furious boy echoed through the room.

"Hey! What did you just say?"

Hinami's blank mask turned to surprise, more shocked than I'd ever seen her. With good reason.

After all, it wasn't Nakamura or one of his crew who had just spoken. It was me.

"Huh?"

Konno glared at me, enraged that one of the rabble had dared to snap at her.

"...What? Tomozaki? Did I say something that offended you? Huh, freak?" she said in the kind of light tone you reserve for the smallest small fry.

"Is 'freak' the only word you people know?" I retorted caustically, forcing myself to return her glare.

"What? Obviously not! Why are you talking to me like that? Ugh, gross!"

"You sure are cocky all of a sudden, Tomozaki. I can barely handle how much of a freak you are right now."

"I mean, why are you protecting him? Come on, it makes zero sense."

"Right? He's not even saying anything! It's hilarious."

"Freaks hang out with freaks, huh? I'll stay away, thanks."

The malice in every one of their words cut through me. I'd lashed out before, but this time, my hands were shaking.

"This is stupid. You wouldn't understand anyway."

"Huh?"

All that tone training, facial expression training, posture training, speech training...for the first time since I started, I understood the point of it. I was nothing compared to these girls when it came to those skills. They'd polished their abilities day in and day out. They could deploy them at will, so much better than me it wasn't even worth comparing us. They knew full well I was nowhere near their level, and they scoffed at me for it. Whatever I said probably wouldn't matter—they weren't going to pay attention to me.

"You know," I began slowly, making my voice as loud and earnest as I could, "there's nothing I hate more than a person who loses and then blames it on the circumstances or the character or something like that instead of making any effort to improve."

"Huh?"

"So what?"

"What's he talking about?"

"Shut the hell up!" I shouted at the top of my voice. "...When I beat Nakamura before, he made excuses. He said it was the character's fault. I thought he was worthless. But what about this time? He lost so bad, in front of all these people, but he didn't make a single excuse! He just kept fighting and fighting! And eventually he took one of my stocks! You people probably have no idea how amazing that is! Not just anyone can do that!"

There are things even I can't overlook.

And what Eriko Konno had said are among them. There was no way I was letting that slide.

"Huh?"

"What's he talking about?"

"I mean, what's the point if you don't win, right?"

"Nakamura doesn't make excuses anymore!"

I took a long breath and screamed my next words.

"But that doesn't matter right now!"

My totally nonsensical words rendered Konno's crew speechless.

I looked Erika Konno straight in the eye. She glared back at me. I was scared, but I refused to look away.

When it came to this, I had guts.

"Konno. You said something a minute ago. You said this game is bullshit."

My level and my equipment were both inadequate for this battle, and I had no way of making up for that. Defeat was staring me in the face, but I refused to give in on this point. These people probably didn't know about story battles, where players don't collapse even when their HP drops to zero. It happens a lot in RPGs.

Of course, even I didn't know if this was one of those!!

"Listen! I hate people who lose and make excuses instead of trying to improve! ...But!"

I poured as much of my genuine personal hatred as possible into the words I screamed next.

"...But I hate people who make fun of *Atafami* even more!!"

Konno's crew had gone completely blank. This was a glaring contest between Konno and me.

"Listen! This is an incredible game! The balance is good. If you practice, there's no limit to how good you can get, and there's no move you can't escape. If you practice enough, there's no combo that can instantly kill you. The characters are all unique and full of ideas. Every one of them could be a main character in another game! The game has plenty of secrets and plenty to do as a solo player, enough to compete with the online mode. And the online environment is outstanding, so you can fight stress-free! The user support is good, too! And! You have normal techniques, but the specials and super-attacks are flashy and fun even if you're not hardcore. *Atafami* combines consideration for hard-core players with the showy effects that casuals like. The two opposites exist in perfect balance. It's an immortal masterpiece!!"

"Huh? You freak. Is that all you wanted to sa—?"

"But absolutely *none* of that matters right now!!"

I screamed so loud my voice started to get hoarse. Even Eriko Konno looked shocked.

"You're so full of shit! What the hell do you mean, 'All your work was pointless'? Don't even try with that BS! You're being a huge bitch, and you don't even know what you're talking about! And I'm not just talking about right now! It's been weeks!! Nakamura's been working his ass off!!"

Nakamura threw me a surprised glance.

"I know what I'm talking about!! Listen to me! That move he used to get out of my combo on the second stock of the second game? It's insanely hard!! Normally, it takes months to master!! And it's even harder to do under pressure like today!! It's not something you do by accident, do you hear me?! And that's not all! The move he used in the last match to spike me? That's a super-hard combo; not even I can nail it every time! It's called MLJ! Moonlight Jail! It's a crazy-hard combo!! He's incredible! Nakamura is incredible, okay?! Clean out your damn ears and listen to me!! You probably wouldn't understand, but Nakamura? He has a goal! Every damn day! He didn't run! He kept going and going and going and going even when he didn't want to! And he achieved this! Maybe it's not the biggest deal! But he got results!!"

I was practically shrieking.

"So stop laughing at him!! Stop laughing at people's hard work!! People who actually work for things? They're doing it right! What they do is something beautiful! More than anyone else, without question!!"

My field of vision was turning white—or black, I couldn't tell.

"I hate people who lose and then make excuses instead of working to improve!! And I hate people who make fun of *Atafami*!! But more than any of that!!"

I kept shouting with everything I had.

"The thing I hate most, in the whole damn world, is idiots like you who don't know how to do *anything* but then have the nerve to laugh at other people's hard work!!"

* * *

Silence. Erika Konno didn't say a word. Her crew watched her. Nakamura stared at me, frozen with surprise. Nakamura's crew fidgeted uncomfortably. Hinami's eyes were moist. *Seriously? Come on.* Hinami was a master actress. Incredible.

The first one to move was Erika Konno.

"…God, what are you even talking about, freak?"

That was the signal for the girls in her crew to come back to life.

"Seriously!"

"Why's he so worked up about a dumb game?"

"What a freak."

It was no good. So this was "the mood." Erika Konno's comment had just established a new rule stating that "taking something seriously is bad." I sensed it with my whole body.

My moment was over. I'd fired every bullet I had. *Hinami, the rest is up to you. I managed to get this far.*

You'd probably have done better.

I glanced at her. She was smiling slightly and nodding. Then she faced forward and opened her lips.

"Actually, I don't think it's such a bad thing—to be serious about something, I mean."

*   *   *

The cheerful, friendly voice echoed through the room.

—Cheerful, friendly, but slightly frightened.

Huh? Frightened?

"...Huh? What do you mean? Yuzu?"

Erika Konno's eyes flashed toward Izumi. *What?! I-Izumi?!*

I looked next to Izumi, where Hinami was standing. Her lips were frozen in an open circle before they had formed any words.

"No, I mean, like... It's a beautiful thing in, like, a boyish kind of way, y'know what I mean...?"

"What? You're defending Tomozaki instead of me?"

A visible shudder shook Izumi's shoulders.

"No, it's not that! But lately, I've been playing *Atafami*—is that what it's called? I've been trying it out, and there's a lot of depth to it! You should try it too, Erika!"

"What? Are you trying to change the subject?"

"N-no, of course not! I mean, he was talking about *Atafami*, right? So like, there's this thing called a short hop, and it's actually really hard. It's hard to get it right! Oh, but I've been getting pretty good at it recently!"

"...Huh?"

It was painful to watch her flounder. Izumi was so good at reading the room; there was no way she didn't know what was happening.

"Plus, it always seems like the strongest techniques take too long to start up, so it's hard to get them right. But I figured something out! First you use one that kicks in quickly, and then you link the strong move from there! That's a combo, right? ...Is that obvious? Ha-ha..."

She was going on pure willpower. It was tough, but she was persevering. On the surface, though, it appeared pretty strange. The crowd was incredibly confused by Yuzu Izumi's awkward struggle and the incomprehensible single-minded franticness of her words. It was like the focus of the scene had blurred.

"Right! So what I'm saying is, Found is a pretty hard character to master. I've got a long way to go. But Foxy is even harder, because, like, he drops faster! And that means he dies from accidents more often. No joke, *Atafami* is hard. I plan to work at it, though. The reason's a secret of course, ha-ha…"

Every person in the room had their eyes on Izumi. For someone who cared so much about what people thought, this had to be excruciating for her.

"Also, when it comes to the other characters…"

Unable to stand it any longer, Hinami took a step forward. But a second before she did, Erika Konno's hand reached Izumi's shoulder.

"Enough already, Izumi. I'm getting bored." She turned to her crew. "Let's get out of here."

The Konno battalion filed out of the room, leaving Izumi behind. Nakamura's crew took that as their opportunity to leave, too.

The door slammed, and for a second the room was silent. Then Izumi collapsed onto the floor.

"…I…I was so scared…!"

She started crying. *Really?*

Nakamura walked over to her. "Hey, what was that all about? It's not like you to push yourself like that."

"But…but…!"

Nakamura put his hand on Izumi's shoulder. *Hey now, don't touch my student without asking first! Oh wait, maybe it's okay, they seem like they're into each other. Yeah, it's fine.*

"Shhh, you don't have to talk about it. You did a good job."

"Ngh…! Shuji…!"

"It's okay now. Hey, you don't want everyone to see you crying, do you?"

Nakamura reached his hand out to Izumi.

"Nuh-uh, I'm okay…!"

Izumi rubbed her tears away fiercely with her sleeve, pulled herself together, and stood up on her own two feet. The two of them walked out of the room…or were about to, when Nakamura turned back and looked sharply at me. In a voice so quiet it barely reached beyond his own mouth, he muttered something. It definitely wasn't loud enough to reach me, but for some reason, I heard it with extreme clarity. As far as I could tell, the will behind it was real.

*   *   *

"Next time, I'll win."

With that, Nakamura and Izumi left the room.

Um...?

"...What just happened?" I said.

"...I have no idea," Hinami answered, gaping. For once, she was defenseless.

As I was looking at her face and trying to piece together the events myself, I realized something.

"Oh, hey..."

"...What?"

"This time..."

I consciously imitated Hinami's favorite ironic tone.

"*You* didn't do a thing."

For the first time since I met Hinami, I could tell from her expression that my words had landed a direct hit.

7

I always want a sequel when the final credits end

It was Saturday, three days after the incident.

Hinami and I were at an Italian place in Kitayono, eating the most delicious salad in the world.

"This is insanely good..."

"Ha-ha. Right?"

Okay, I might've expected the pasta or pizza to blow me away, but not the appetizer salad. An attack from an unexpected angle. Very sneaky. Too sneaky. But I was happy about it.

As I reveled in the perfect harmony of the dressing and the natural sweetness of the vegetables, we began our usual meeting. I'd have preferred to talk to her right away, but she had been concentrating on getting the situation back under control, and this was the first time she was able to make time for a real conversation.

"But anyway, it really was terrible..."

The scene that unfolded in the former principal's office was so dramatic and had been witnessed by so many people that tons of kids at school had heard every last detail. They knew about Nakamura's string of losses, my cocky comments, my freakishly high level of play, my heartfelt tirade, my...huh? Pretty much everything was a criticism of me. Ha-ha-ha.

But the impact on the class power structure had been...surprisingly minor.

As always, Nakamura reigned at the top of the hierarchy, and no visible battle occurred between his group and Erika Konno's. Of course, the groups didn't hang out as often anymore, but on Friday, I saw Izumi mediating in a slightly awkward conversation between Nakamura and Konno.

They really were ridiculously good at repairing interpersonal relationships. Seemed they were just seeing how things progressed and waiting for a full recovery.

While all that was going on, two major changes took place.

The first had to do with Izumi. Practically the whole class figured out that she'd been practicing *Atafami* so that Nakamura would pay attention to her, and the general attitude was that her efforts were heartwarming. Nakamura might have been the only person in class who didn't realize how she felt. "Dense" was becoming his class nickname, and his obliviousness to that, too, became a joke in itself. He was too wrapped up in *Atafami*. If he was that competitive, he just might have a gift for gaming.

The second change had to do with Nakamura. After the incident, he got even more into *Atafami*, maybe because he hated losing to me. That alone would have been fine, but he didn't care at all if people thought it was weird. Seems he'd taken to using even short breaks and lunchtime to practice like a man possessed.

In other words, it was like...I was supposed to serve as Cupid's arrow, but as it turned out, I actually caused him to pay more attention to *Atafami* than to Izumi... *Nakamura, you used to pay a fair amount of attention to Izumi, didn't you? Um, sorry. Guess my plan backfired.*

"Well, all in all, I'm glad the damage to you was limited."

"...Yeah, I guess you're right."

It's true. The impact of all this on me was smaller than I imagined.

The incident took place on Wednesday, which meant I had two days of school between then and now. A handful of my classmates were born-and-bred rubberneckers, and they asked me a lot of questions, but most of them did it out of simple curiosity rather than good or bad intentions. When I answered with the truth, they'd say something like "Wow!" and walk off, satisfied. The whole confrontation didn't make me any new enemies. Then again, it didn't make me any new friends, either.

But I think the main reason Nakamura and I didn't suffer more damage was because Hinami was running interference for us behind the scenes.

She missed both of our after-school meetings. All she said by way of explanation was that she had "some stuff to do," but I witnessed her spreading good PR for Nakamura several times during that period. The time I remember best was when she cheerfully announced to the class, "Wow! But if Shuji is that crazy about *Atafami*, it must be fun!" Guess that's what they call "stealth marketing." She was sneakily manipulating the impression people had of Nakamura and *Atafami*.

I'm fairly sure she was doing the same for me...and for that I was grateful.

Also, this may have been happening before, or I may have just noticed it because of that conversation we had, but one time I heard her enthusiastically say "Hexactly!" in front of a classmate. She really does like that phrase.

"Anyway, what else do you want to hear about?" I asked.

"Aside from that whole mess before...there's Fuka-chan."

"Right. Well, a bunch of stuff happened."

I told her about admitting the truth and not inviting her to the movie. Hinami sighed with exasperation.

"You mean to tell me you had two good prospects, and you let both of them slip away? Honestly, do you even want to do this?"

"Of course I do!"

"...Well, no use crying over spilled milk. Let's think about what to do next." With that, she began cooking up a plan.

"...Right," I said, once again appreciating her powers.

This was where she excelled. For some reason, I had taken it for granted that she was amazing and never thought about *why* she was so amazing.

The answer was actually simple. She was amazing because she made a huge effort to be that way. She faced reality and buckled down to work, moving forward one step at a time, propelled by her own will.

And it was incredible.

I'd fully realized it after I'd heard the file on the voice recorder. Ever since, I'm not sure how to put it, but I'd felt something like respect or awe for her.

And that made me want to start taking initiative beyond her instructions.

"Hey...this is off topic, but..."

"What?"

I brushed my hand over my inner pocket and tried to make my comment as innocently as possible.

"You know that premiere of the Mari Joan film tomorrow? Well, how about we go together?"

Hinami looked confused for a second. Then she smirked and said, just as innocently, "Oh, I'm sorry. I have plans tomorrow. I can't go."

I made an effort to brush it off with a laugh, but then I genuinely crumpled. I didn't stand a chance.

"But, well…," she said.

"…What?"

She gave me a kind but playful smile, like a parent watching over her dull child.

"I'm free after this. Do you want to go to a different movie?"

For a second, my mind went blank.

After that, a feeling of excitement that was almost like elation or accomplishment overtook me. I'm not exactly sure why I felt that way, but I don't think it had to do with getting close to a normie or going out with a girl. I think it was the primal elation that comes from working hard and getting the results you want in the real world, plain and simple. I'm not positive, but that's what I suspect.

"…Hexactly!" I said, trying out Hinami's favorite phrase for myself. She pointed out that I wasn't quite using it correctly. *Huh. Guess that's another area for improvement.*

But that's what life's all about, right? Well, I'll show her a thing or two.

I may be a beginner at this game, but I'm about to get serious.

—By bottom-tier character nanashi, the best noob gamer in Japan

Afterword

Greetings. Yuki Yaku here, first-time author and undeserving recipient of the 10th Shogakukan Light Novel Grand Prize.

Of course, I didn't create this book published by Gagaga Bunko alone; many people have collaborated to make it a reality. I hope that I can at the very least express my thoughts honestly and straightforwardly in this entirely superfluous afterword.

That said, talking about myself isn't one of my strengths, and describing the content and themes of the novel would basically be taking away space for independent analysis and making demands on the book after it's already left my hands, so I figured I'd talk about my initial feelings when I saw the cover illustration instead.

When I received the illustration from the editor in charge of cover art, my first reaction was surprise at how cute it was. There was so much to admire: the energetic, determined expression on Hinami's face, the light texture of her hair, the fetishism evoked by the placement of the schoolbag and blazer... But the part that got me the most was the depiction of her thighs. (I will leave discussion of additional points to future opportunities, which I am sure will present themselves.)

As for what exactly I found so moving about those thighs, well, the answer is quite simple. It was the hip joint of her left leg (the right side from the viewer's perspective). Now that I've said this much, half my readers will probably be nodding in understanding. Yes, dear readers, your guess is correct. I am speaking of the swell of her hip.

I don't know whether it would be better to call it flesh or the gush of youth, but the round swelling in the area of her hip joint really got me.

At that juncture, however, I composed myself and examined this leg starting at the knee by tracing the line up to the thigh, which brought about a realization. The line starts out concave, expressing the slimness and suppleness of the leg, but the moment it reaches the hip joint, just past where her hands are planted on the ground, it rounds outward.

An electric shock ran through my brain.

I had sensed viscerally just how much intention this choice of a few millimeters contained. My analysis may have been uninvited, but nevertheless I was quite confident that it was correct.

There was a reason for my confidence. That is, you can draw thighs on a stick figure, too. In case my meaning is not immediately clear, let me explain. Once you've drawn the head, body, and lower legs on a stick figure, and made a bend for the knees, the area above this bend will automatically become the thighs. If you tell someone those sticks are thighs, no one will complain. At the very least, I won't.

In other words, if the illustrator had simply wanted to express the fact that these were Hinami's thighs, he could have done so with a stick figure. He could even have gone a little further and enclosed the area in straight lines and colored in a skin tone, and that would have been more than enough.

But the cover illustrator for this project was Fly, and Fly decided not only to add curves to those thighs, but to give them the most delicate of contours. The purpose of this innovation was to add realism to the picture and infuse it with a very particular allure—no, those roundabout phrases are no good. The purpose was simply to lend warmth to Hinami through the magic of a few millimeters.

I urge those of you reading the paperback version to turn to the cover, and those of you reading the ebook to bring up the cover on your screen, and gently touch those thighs with your finger. Your pointer finger is probably best. Well, what do you think? Do you feel it? Do you feel that certain warmth—the warmth of Hinami?

At the very least, I feel it. Right now I am touching both thighs with the tip of my right pointer finger as I type with my left hand. Certainly, that warmth is slightly different from the physical warmth one experiences when actually touching someone. It is different. I accept that. Nevertheless, a warmth breathes beneath my fingertips—so faintly I almost can't feel it, but it's real.

I hope that I have succeeded in communicating my feelings.

And now on to the acknowledgements.

First, thank you to everyone involved in the selection of this book for the 10th Shogakukan Light Novel Grand Prize, as well as those who assisted with its editing, publishing, marketing, and sales.

Second, thank you to my editor Iwaasa, who gave me so much severe yet sincere advice; to my roommate T, who read the manuscript before I submitted it to the contest and helped me revise it through valuable and candid comments; and to Fly, the illustrator, who contributed so many surprisingly cute and sexy illustrations to this work of a complete unknown.

Finally, thank you to everyone who reads this book. I hope you will join me for future volumes.

Yuki Yaku